I spun the targeting head. The little rooftop mounting rotated on glass-smooth gimbals, giving me a right-eye view of the scene behind us. Recoil from the automatic cannon had flipped Platt's car, just like I figured it would. CHINLESS WONDER rolled off the road with boxed ammo popping like the 4th of July.

The next two Pirate cars were pulling around their burning leaders. I saw somebody jump out of I'M BAD, but flames wrapped the body so I couldn't tell whether it was Jack or his late girlfriend. 20mm ammunition exploded, tossing fragments high in the air.

I thought we were headed straight into town. Even without the flywheel's power boost. THE SQUARE DEAL was obviously faster than the Pirates' junkers. None of the survivors would push it, not after what had happened to their friends.

Instead, JC screamed, "Target a driver and hang on!" THE SQUARE DEAL hunkered down on her suspension as JC threw the car into a screaming turn that seemed to spin us in our own length.

I couldn't believe that forward momentum didn't flip us off the road—

But driving wasn't my business, targets were.

Tor Books by David Drake

Birds of Prey
Bridgehead
Cross the Stars
The Dragon Lord
The Forlorn Hope
Fortress
From the Heart of Darkness
The Jungle
Killer (with Karl Edward Wagner)
Skyripper
Time Safari

CAR WARRIORS™ #1

DAVID DRAKE
THE SQUARE DEAL

A TOM DOHERTY ASSOCIATES BOOK
NEW YORK

This is a work of fiction. All the characters and events portrayed in this book are fictitious, and any resemblance to real people or events is purely coincidental.

CAR WARRIORS: THE SQUARE DEAL

Copyright © 1992 by David Drake

Car Wars and Car Warriors are registered trademarks of Steve Jackson Games Incorporated, used under license. All characters in this book are the property of Steve Jackson Games Incorporated.

Cover art by John Zeleznik
Maps by John M. Ford

A Tor Book
Published by Tom Doherty Associates, Inc.
175 Fifth Avenue
New York, N.Y. 10010

Tor ® is a registered trademark of Tom Doherty Associates, Inc.

ISBN: 0-812-51989-2

First edition: September 1992

Printed in the United States of America

0 9 8 7 6 5 4 3 2 1

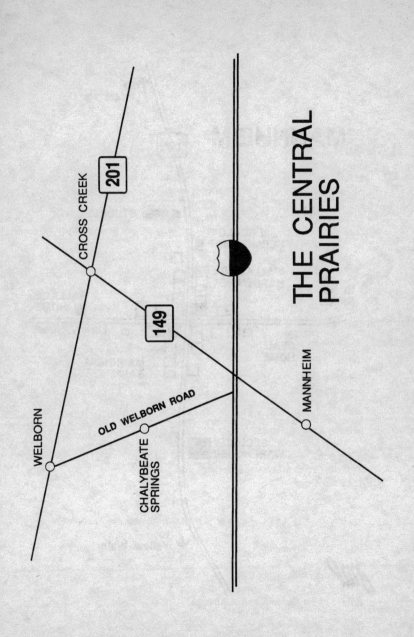

THE CENTRAL
PRAIRIES

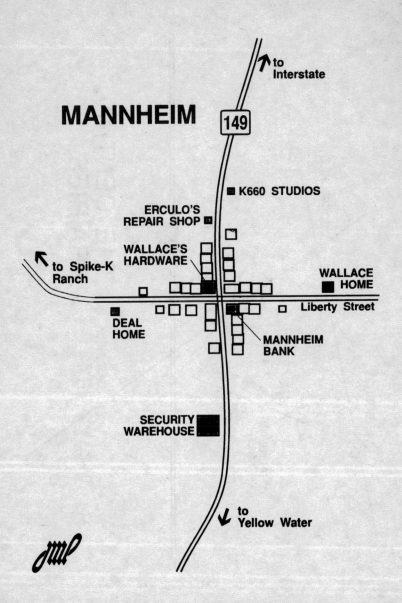

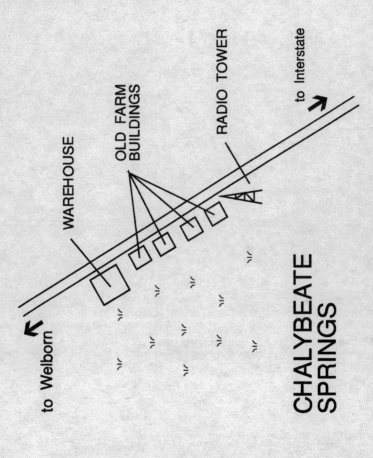

to Welborn

WAREHOUSE

OLD FARM
BUILDINGS

RADIO TOWER

to Interstate

CHALYBEATE
SPRINGS

CHAPTER 1

A data line at the bottom of the monitor screen ran the specs of the rig whose feed I watched in the production room of K660, *The Eyes of the Central Prairie Here in Mannheim.* The turret on the trailer mounted a cal fifty coaxial with a seventy-five mike-mike recoilless. The long-nose tractor itself carried a rocket pod on each front fender. The rockets' fifty-pound warheads were guaranteed to discourage roadblocks *real* quick, especially since they were backed up by the 40mm automatic cannon in the turret on the cab roof.

The data crawl didn't tell me whether the cab turret was separately manned or if the forty was remotely controlled from either the back turret or the driver—who had his hands full already, State 149 not being a real featherbed of a road. Whichever, considering the rig's armor and considerable weight of droppable weapons, there was no way in Hades the bike gang following a mile back could pose a serious threat.

So why *were* the dirtballs following?

"Brian?" called Ditsy Wallace from the editing bay, where she faced a bank of monitors showing arena footage. Flames and the quick twinkle of muzzle flashes reflected from the lustrous black of her long hair. "If you're going to hang around, you can at least be useful. Come here and help me choose clips for tomorrow morning's Sports Highlights."

Ditsy was my age, eighteen, but she seemed a lot older. It wasn't just her father's money, though there was that too. Big Ben Wallace owned K660, owned Wallace's Hardware, *and* the Mannheim Bank, *and* Security Warehouse—and a lot of the rest of Mannheim through bank loans, real estate, and personal property.

When you own everything a man has, you're likely to start thinking you own the man himself; and chances are, the man feels that way about it, too.

"Ditsy," I said, "I think you ought to take a look at this local feed. Something funny's going on."

"News?" she said. She was beside me in an instant, moving as quickly and gracefully as a cat pouncing. Ditsy could have been a prime duelist if she'd wanted to train for it, but the only thing that interested her was TV. She had her heart set on anchoring a major market. Knowing how good she was—and how driven—I figured she'd get there, and sooner rather than later.

Nobody was interested in what Brian Deal's heart was set on. If anybody'd asked me, though, I might have said, "On Ditsy Wallace."

"We're getting the feed from a solo," I said aloud, "but there's a pair of trucks five miles ahead."

I typed commands into the console, splitting the monitor screen. The camera in the rear turret continued to feed a view of the bike gang onto the right side of the screen, but the left half showed the fuzzy running lights of a distant rig as seen from the cab turret.

"There's a sedan, too, in between," I added. "The two rigs up front passed it a few miles back. It's gray, so it doesn't show up."

Ditsy frowned at the monitor. "There's just eight of the dirtballs?" she said.

"Maybe ten," I hedged. "But not enough to knock over a rig by themself."

"They must have a roadblock set up ahead," Ditsy said decisively. She cut on the monitor beside the one I was using. "Do we have a feed from the lead rigs?"

"Negative," I said, glad I'd already checked that. "They're Blaskie Express. But I don't see logrollers trying to bite off three rigs at a time, either. That's about as survivable as jumping on a live grenade."

K660 was willing to buy the video feed from any vehicle running within a hundred miles of the station. That was Ditsy's idea, giving some real backbone to the station's motto— *The Eyes of the Central Prairie*. The signals were bounced to a comsat and then downloaded through the microwave link on the station roof.

Mostly the feeds were crap: bad road, alkaline prairie, and a lot of cows—exactly what folks around here saw every time they looked out a window. Now and again there was a shootup that was worth airing for local interest, even if it didn't amount to a hill of beans compared to commercial footage the station could have run instead. People liked to see their own kin and neighbors, especially if the locals smoked some out-of-town tourist.

Gypsy truckers were glad to supply video. The access fee the station paid was nominal, and the use fee—in the rare instance the feed actually got on the air—wasn't a fortune either. On the other hand, it was a little something toward the costs of running a rig—and a lot of truckers didn't mind the thought of being famous either.

Most of the big firms took another line, though. They figured their jobs—and their profits—were in transporting freight. Anything that glamorized goons who dueled on the highways cost the Brotherhood money and lives. K660 got no videos from them.

In fact, Ditsy had had to buy an up-armored mobile unit for K660 right after she started her local service. The previous vehicle, a brightly painted box with a cherrypicker camera crane on the roof and a mini-studio inside, had been swept off the road by a Blaskie Express rig whose tail gunner then put a short burst through the powerplant with his Gatling.

Nothing personal. Just a little warning about how the big firms felt regarding K660's new policy.

"Do we have audio?" Ditsy asked. She plugged her right-ear-only headset into the console next to mine and keyed a frequency search without taking her eyes off the monitor.

The rig feeding us began to accelerate, and it looked as though the leading pair had throttled back slightly. The truckers didn't know what was going on either. They'd decided to form a tighter convoy, hoping that would scrape the dirt off the heels of the last-in-line.

"There was just hash the last time I checked," I told Ditsy. "They're still fifty miles north of Mannheim, and the atmospherics aren't helping CB propagation tonight."

The sedan had slowed also, keeping a constant three miles or so behind the leading pair of rigs. Though it was growing in the cab-turret feed, the civilian's smoke-gray paint job blurred the smaller vehicle into the background.

I thought I saw a ruby glimmer from the tiny turret on the roof of the sedan. If I was right, the civilian had used a laser rangefinder to paint the rig which bore up behind him at an increasing rate of speed.

Ranging other traffic, especially ranging a heavily armed rig, was rarely a good idea and frequently a suicidal one. Under the circumstances, a civilian in a spitball special could be expected to do dumb things in panic when he found himself sandwiched between rigs squeezing closer. It just showed the poor sucker understood the situation.

Ditsy stopped fooling with the audio. She reached over to my keyboard and typed just the command I was afraid she would enter. The data line on the monitor switched from the rig's armament to its identification:

SPIKE-K SPECIAL #114. KOKO TALBERT/DRIVER.

And that, so far as Ditsy was concerned, was all she wrote.

"Shut it off!" she snapped as she pulled her headset out of the console. She turned her back so abruptly that the ends of her long black hair popped as they swayed behind her.

"Ditsy, something's going on here—" I said.

She turned again. I'd seen her angry before; often enough at me, because I didn't come up to speed fast enough or didn't have the go-for-the-throat drive she demanded from herself and anybody she liked—

Because I was pretty sure she liked me regardless.

But I hadn't often seen her *this* angry before.

"Listen to me, Brian!" she said in a voice like glass

breaking. "Stannard Kames and his Spike-K operation aren't news on this station. Do you understand? Not unless they all die and go to Hell, where they belong! Now, turn that off and come help me—or get out and don't come back!"

"I'm sorry, Ditsy," I said. "I should have told you."

But (not that I said it aloud) I was right. A handful of dirtball bikers chasing fully-armed rigs was *weird*, and weird meant news.

I knew why Ditsy was mad. I'd been there when it happened: when five Spike-K cowboys in light pickups decided to pay back Big Ben Wallace for some of K660's editorials.

I live with my mom on the west edge of town. Liberty Street's paved pretty much as far as our house, but from there on out it isn't maintained, except that once in a while Spike-K cowboys dumped gravel in the worst of the potholes.

That's all there was west of here: the Spike-K Ranch. Stannard Kames didn't like anybody around except folks he owned. Back when first we moved to Mannheim when I was five, there were still a few independent ranchers rounding up salable herds from the cattle running wild since the Collapse.

Not anymore. Some of the independents had moved away. Some went to work for the Spike-K; I heard that Stannard Kames treated his people pretty decent, so long as they remembered to treat *him* like God Almighty.

Some of the independents were too stiff-necked to run or bend. There's a lot of empty land hereabouts, and men are buried under more than one piece of it.

Kames had a regular little empire, which included his own trucks to carry much of the ranch's supplies and dressed meat. Still, the Spike-K needed Mannheim, and it stuck in Stannard Kames' craw that he couldn't own the town outright.

Because Big Ben Wallace already did.

I'd never say it to Ditsy, but the reason her dad and Stannard Kames hated each other so was that they were too much alike. Things smoldered on for a long while like a fire in a coal seam, not quite breaking the surface. Kames tightened his grip on the cattle business, while Big Ben Wallace bought up the town and loaned money to all the fenced-crop farmers between here and Welborn, north of the Interstate.

Then Big Ben started running editorials on K660, right in prime time, saying the only use for cowboys was fertilizer and even then they stank up the soil. I don't think he meant a whole lot by it—just a little prod at Stannard Kames, who didn't own a TV station to get back at him.

Three nights later, Big Ben walked out of the station as his chauffeured car pulled up in front to carry him home. Five Spike-K pickups passed, accelerating down State 149, and sprayed the car with yellow paint. The trucks were high-sprung off-roaders. Two of them bounced up on the sidewalk to make sure they got full coverage. They took off at full honk, into Mannheim proper and then west for home on Liberty Street.

What Big Ben should have done was go back inside the station, have his car cleaned—and maybe wait till he cooled down to decide whether or not he really wanted to push things farther with the Spike-K. Instead, he hopped into his car and screamed at his chauffeur to get after those scum-suckers *now*!

Big Ben could afford the best. He rode a gas-powered Grenadier luxury model with heavy armor and a pod of laser-guided missiles on a disappearing mount that didn't spoil the lines of his car. Because the mount wasn't deployed when the cowboys made their statement, the paint hadn't done it any harm. The shutter of the stabilized targeting laser was gummed shut, though.

7

The chauffeur had a palm-sized patch of clear windshield to see out of and he had to twist to use that, but he wasn't dumb enough to tell his boss they ought to sit tight. Big Ben raised the missile launcher and bent over the backup optical periscope built into the mount.

I was sitting in front of our house, wishing I was somewhere else and some*body* else, when the pickups went by like sparrows chased by a hawk. When they hit the gravel, they raised a dust cloud better than any smokescreen, but I didn't guess it was going to help much. Big Ben's car was right behind them, already doing twice the pickups' best speed and still accelerating.

Big Ben fired as he came on. The backblast from the launcher was a yellow flash. The *crack* of each missile going supersonic was right on top of the dull *whump* of ignition—but before I heard any sound, the warhead had already raised a column of dirt well down the road ahead of the intended targets.

It's next to impossible to hit somebody at any range with an unstabilized weapon when both of you are bouncing over potholes. Besides, Big Ben was a businessman, not a duelist. Pretty quick, though, the car's superior speed was going to put its ram plate in the cowboys' back pockets. The Grenadier carried a reload pod for the launcher, and at point-blank range, the missiles would put paid to the jokers from the Spike-K.

One after another, the pickups went airborne. They were so close together that it looked like a circus act. One of the trucks got crossed up in the air. The driver managed to save it after all, though the fishtail when he landed back on the gravel looked like a bomb blast.

On their way in town, the ranch hands had removed the

culvert where the road crossed a dry wash. Their light off-road vehicles hopped it safely. The heavy car behind them nosed into the far side of the gully and flipped end-for-end at least six times. Then the gas tank exploded, and the dust cloud didn't settle for half an hour.

Spectacular isn't the word. The wreck would have made national TV if there'd been anybody around to film it; but there was only me, thirteen-year-old Brian Deal, with my mom crying for me to get inside before a stray bullet blew my fool head off.

The Grenadier had first-rate crash protection. The airbag collapsed so the steering column impaled the chauffeur after the third or fourth impact, but Big Ben came through the whole business alive . . . only with a broken back, and no use of his legs ever again.

Big Ben Wallace had always hated Kames and the Spike-K Ranch. After the wreck, I think Ditsy hated them even more than her father did.

"Okay, Ditsy," I said with a last regretful glance toward the screen. "What d'ye want in particular for Sports Highlights?"

The studio phone rang before my hand reached the monitor's kill switch. I lunged for the handset, because I knew who it would be. Ditsy was closer and got to the phone first. The smile she gave me as she listened was hard and emotionless. "Yes, he's here, Mrs. Deal," she said. "I'll put him on."

Ditsy could have spit as she gave me the handset and it wouldn't have made me feel any lower.

"Mom, *please*!" I hissed into the phone. "I've told you not to call me here!"

"Brian, you know how I worry about you walking home

9

so late at night," my mother said in that sad, calm tone that made me want to climb the walls. She'd never raised her voice to me, but whenever I did something wrong—and "wrong" the way Mom defined it was "anything that made it seem like Brian had a life of his own"—she sounded like I'd been whipping her with barbed wire.

"Mom, I'll be all right," I said, trying to pitch my voice low enough that Ditsy couldn't hear. She was facing the bank of arena images again, pretending she didn't know what was going on. "I've got my grenade launcher, and—"

"You're all I've got, Brian, ever since my John left me," Mom plowed on, following a script I must have heard once a week in the twelve years since my brother drove away from the house and disappeared. "It's not safe to walk at night, you *know* that, and my heart just freezes until I see you're home safe."

"Then let me buy a car, Mom!" I said. "I can afford one now with my job. Erculo would sell me a fix-up—"

"Oh, Brian," Mom moaned. "So that you can go off and leave me without so much as a call in twelve years like your brother John? Is that what you want?"

Sometimes, Mom, that's just what I want. Aloud I said, "Mom, I'm going to hang up, now. I'll be home soon. If you call back again tonight, I'll never come home again. I swear it."

I think I meant it. I could sleep the night in Erculo's shop, and the next morning there was bound to be a rig going somewhere with room in a blister for a kid with a lot of simulator experience although none of the real thing.

Mom heard something in my tone, anyhow, because she said, "You don't know how you hurt me when you act like this, Brian, darling," like she was heartbroken. But she hung up, and that was what I wanted as much as anything I could imagine right then.

I put the handset down. "I'm sorry, Ditsy—" I started to say.

She turned around sharply. "Yes, you're always sorry, aren't you, Brian?" she said. "Maybe someday you'll manage to be *something* instead of just being sorry, sorry, sorry!"

I don't know what I would have said then—maybe nothing, just picked up my grenade launcher and walked out the door. But that was when it happened on the monitor.

The bike gang was still a pattern of distant shadows on the right side of the split screen. They hadn't come any closer to the truck during the time I'd been on the phone with Mom.

On the left split, the leading rigs were within a mile and a half of the cab-turret camera. The gray sedan was only about 500 yards off the front bumper. I reached for the monitor switch again, thinking that the civilian car was going to have a rough time from the bikers unless it closed up tighter to the rigs than it'd done so far.

The sedan, its stabilized laser target probe painting the Spike-K rig, swapped ends in what looked like no more than its own length.

"Ditsy!" I shouted.

I'd never seen anything turn like that from highway speed. Even if the tires managed to grip—and they did—G-forces must have slammed back the driver as if he were in a centrifuge. The TV image of the smoke-gray sedan swelled for an instant as the cab gunner tried to sight on a vehicle he'd pretty much ignored for fear of the bikers and what they might be chasing the rig into.

He was too late.

There was an open gunport in the center of the sedan's

nose. As the stubby gray vehicle swung to bear on the Spike-K rig, the port spewed a bottle-shaped flare: plasma, atoms stripped of their electrons by a jolt of electricity. The fluorescent, yellow-orange cloud hid the sedan momentarily.

For an instant, the trailer camera held a steady image of the bikers while the image from the cab bucked skyward. Then both cameras oscillated wildly as the rig jackknifed. Both halves of the screen blanked within a fraction of a second of one another.

I let out my breath slowly. Ditsy stood beside me, professionally interested again.

"Brian?" she asked. "Did you shut off the feed?"

"No," I said, "somebody else did. He fired one shot. And he took out a fully armored rig."

CHAPTER 2

The most unusual thing about the white sedan that drove past the crash site was just that: the driver slowed only enough to pass between the wreck and our tow truck across the road. Then he breezed on down State 149 toward Mannheim instead of rubbernecking like most folks, hoping to see blood.

There was plenty of blood if they knew where to look. The driver's body, the big pieces of it, was under a tarp waiting for a crew from the Spike-K ranch to pick up. I was the guy who was going to have to sponge out the cab, though, after Erculo and I towed the rig back to the shop.

The tail gunner was under the tarp also. She'd been killed cleanly in the crash, but a biker had worked her body over with a length of triple-row primary chain.

I thought about bike gangs in Erculo's simulator—neat electronic figures that flipped or exploded in the simulator's

13

sight picture. I'd never shot at anybody for real. I wanted to, now that I'd seen the woman's body.

"Gimme twenty inches of Fibrex, Erculo," I called from where I balanced over the hitch. The trailer lay on its side, while the tractor had landed top down in the yellowish alkaline soil, but they were still coupled. That was the first thing we had to take care of before we towed the two parts of the rig in separately.

Half a dozen cars pulled alongside the wreck, spinning up their motors out of gear. They had fins welded to the driveshaft housings on their undersides to amplify the rotary whine into a high-pitched squeal. I kept my back turned.

"Hey, Deadeye!" Jack Terry called from the lead car, with I'M BAD painted across the hood. "Did you do this yerse'f?"

"Move along, Terry," boomed Lynx Feldshuh through the public address speaker in the front turret of his police van. "Now—or I unblock the road myself."

Strictly speaking, Lincoln Feldshuh was town marshal, so this stretch of highway was outside his jurisdiction. The Lynx wasn't the sort who spent a lot of time on legal niceties; and anyhow, just about the whole town of Mannheim was parked up and down 149, guessing about what had happened—and how.

"Sure, Marshal," Jack called over the nail-scraping whine of his car. "Just talking to my friend Deadeye here. I figure he's the only feller around could've made a kill like this, don't you?"

The hydraulic traverse of the police van's front turret purred. Jack got the message. He slammed I'M BAD into gear and led his pack away to find parking off the road.

Jack Terry and his gang, the Pirates, were wannabes from

14

Mannheim and the farms east of here. Maybe I'd have been one if Mom had let me have a car, but I hope I wouldn't ever have been that stupid.

Their cars were junk. "Bolt-on specials," Erculo called them sneeringly, but they were worse than that. None of the gang could afford proper custom work. They bought bits and pieces from wrecks, then attached the parts to their cars with clamps, bad welds, and baling wire.

Jack had reaper blades bolted to the front fenders of I'M BAD. He wasn't nearly as bad as he was dumb. He'd mounted a 20mm Gatling gun where the passenger seat had been so that it could fire out through a hole in the front grille.

Since the chassis came from a compact, a burst from so powerful a gun mounted off the centerline would throw the little car right off the road. Heck, a *long* burst would spin I'M BAD like a top, though I didn't think the Gatling would get off more than a few rounds before jamming. The mount wasn't solid enough.

Jack had two machine guns firing through side ports in the back. Usually one of the younger Pirates or Jack's current girlfriend rode in a jumpseat to load them, but the firing switch was on the steering wheel. I'd seen him plenty times outside of town, cutting brodies and spraying the landscape with the machine guns.

The other five cars were pretty much the same—or worse. Billy Bristow had managed to sling an ancient 105mm recoilless rifle under the jacked-up chassis of a mid-size. I *know* he'd never tried to fire the big gun, because the backblast of the recoilless rifle would have blown the whole rear end of his car a hundred yards down the road.

Billy had tried to make a deflector baffle out of sheet metal, but anybody with half a brain could see it was inadequate. The vents required to make a recoilless rifle work on a vehicle double the weight of the installation and slow the rate of fire way down, because of the extra metal that has to be swung out of the way in order to load. Billy's gun was pure brag, but he and his little brother Ben rode their DRAGON WAGON like they were real kings of the hill.

Weapons were sexy, so Terry and the Pirates had guns and drop-packages attached to every corner of their cars. Their armor was a hodgepodge, bolted on in chunks. Some of it was pretty heavy, taken from tractor cabs and the plating of wrecked luxury cars, but the attachments weren't sturdy enough to stand up to serious gunfire. You don't have to penetrate armor if the welds holding a plate crack and drop it when hit by the first shot of a burst.

Like I say, stupid wannabes in stupid cars. But the fact remained, they *had* cars; and I didn't.

I guess I better explain "Deadeye." Erculo does custom work as well as normal repairs. Two years ago, I'd helped him fit a helmet-mounted laser link to the 2.75-inch rocket pod on the car of a local farmer. The fellow's kids were grown and living on their own, so he wanted hands-off guidance when he didn't have a gunner aboard. The helmet system aimed the rocket wherever the wearer focused the red dot on the lens of his right goggle.

Or it was supposed to. We tested the system on the range behind Erculo's shop. There were a lot of spectators, Terry and the Pirates included, because fourteen-pound warheads make an impressive show when they go off.

So there I was in the driver's seat, proud as could be, with the farmer sitting beside me and what looked like the whole town watching. I cranked the car to power up the systems, laid the red dot in my eyepiece on the wrecked sedan a full 500 yards away, and said, "Watch *this*!" to the farmer as I toggled off the first rocket.

It ripped out of the pod and hit the ground maybe thirty feet ahead of our bumper. The whole windshield flashed orange when the warhead burst. The spectators flattened, but that just made them bigger targets for all the dirt and trash that flew up from the blast crater.

Some of those rocks were the size of a man's head. I know, because one of them bounced off the hood right in front of me, while the farmer screamed that I was wrecking his car. Truth to tell, the blast *hadn't* done the finish much good.

Erculo got to his feet while dirt was still raining down. He shouted for me to get out, that something was wrong. I was too rattled to think straight; and anyway, I couldn't believe what had happened.

"It's okay!" I said. I stuck the red dot smack in the middle of the target, took a deep breath, and fired another round.

BLAM! Right into the crater from the first one.

Erculo grabbed me by the shoulder and dragged me out of the car. That was a good thing, because I was so spooked I might have done the same thing with the other five rockets as well.

It took Erculo and me six hours to figure out the problem. The system had been misassembled at the factory. The reticle of the optical sight was installed upside down. Instead of correcting for parallax between the eyepiece and the rocket pod on the car roof, it doubled the error.

Not our fault. Not *my* fault. But that story had made me "Deadeye" forever after in Mannheim.

"Here you go, Brian," Erculo called. I turned, and he

tossed me a short roll of Fibrex explosive with a ten-second detonator. "But I think you need more, do you not?"

Erculo's a good boss and the best friend I had in Mannheim, Ditsy excepted—when she was in a good mood. He's a short, stocky guy, as bald as if he'd been scalped. Town rumor was that he'd run with a bike gang until one of his buddies gouged out his right eye.

Maybe that was true, maybe not. All I knew was that Erculo kept to himself—that he treated me decent, better than decent, as soon as he realized I really cared about learning what he had to teach me—and that he was as good a mechanic as you were likely to find between Chicago and the Coast.

Erculo could have written his own ticket with any top-rated dueling team. Why he didn't, well, I guess that's his own affair.

I began to wrap Fibrex around the kingpin. When the rig jackknifed, the big rod attaching the semi to the tractor's fifth wheel had bent at nearly 90°. It could no longer be released normally.

"I think this much'll do, boss," I said. "You wouldn't believe how the sucker's torqued. It won't take much of a bang to finish the job, and we don't want to do any more damage ourselves, right?"

Erculo snorted, but the principle was one he'd hammered into me in the first few months I'd been helping him at the shop. The thermite grenade the bikers had set on the hood as they fled hadn't ignited—a bad fuze—but that didn't matter either. As a practical matter, I could have used a ton of the coarse, gray explosive cloth and not made a real difference to the salvage value. A rig that had taken as much damage as this one—partly from the hijacker's shot, but mostly as a result of the high-speed crash itself—was irreparable junk.

But that was a decision for the owner to make. Erculo's job—under contract from the State Department of Highways—was to tow in the wreck and keep the road clear. A twenty-by-four inch strip of Fibrex would split the load into packets our wrecker could handle. I tied the explosive carefully around the bent kingpin and pinned the detonator to the center of the knot.

I glanced around. Erculo was already shooing spectators clear. I pulled the pin of the detonator and shouted, "Fire in the hole!" as I jumped down to shelter behind the cab.

Ten seconds seems forever when you know there's going to be an explosion at the end of it. By the time the sharp *crack* came and the wreck shuddered, I'd about decided the detonator was a dud.

That was when Stannard Kames and the Spike-K crew arrived.

They weren't as quick as I'd expected, but I guess Kames didn't want to show up until he'd gathered the kind of backing he thought he might need. He'd brought a dozen all-wheel-drive pickups and about thirty men. Four of the heavier pickups carried turreted shelltops, but I think Kames' own black six-by-six, CHIEF, was the only one that mounted heavy weapons as a matter of course.

They came up 149 from the south, three abreast. That meant they were scraping cars parked on the shoulder as they got nearer the wreck. The cattlemen's pickups weren't going to get marked up worse than they would in a normal day chivying steers. As for other folks—Stannard Kames wasn't a peaceful man at the best of times, and the hijacking wouldn't have improved his disposition. Nobody uttered a peep about a scratch in their paintwork.

"Boy," said Erculo in a low voice, "we have work to do. Fix the hooks."

He was right; and anyway, he was the boss. I took the drag lines and clambered onto the overturned tractor to attach them. We had to get it wheel-side down again before we could tow it in.

Car doors thumped shut as spectators decided to watch whatever happened next from behind armor. I risked a glance over my shoulder and saw the blue-and-white police van nose out onto the road to block the Spike-K caravan. The Lynx must have been on the console controlling the forward turret—the flamethrower and coaxial machine gun—because his deputy, Hannah Martin, was driving.

Nobody around here knew quite what to think of the red-haired deputy marshal. Hannah was on the tall side for a woman, with a hard, rangy body and a smile that could crack rocks. She'd either come from a big city or wanted it to be thought that she had, because she sure didn't dress like the local girls.

Today was typical. In the driver's seat of the van, she wore black leather slacks and an off-the-bosom top beneath transparent body armor. I guess she must have been at least thirty years old, but her exposed left breast looked as firm as an apple.

I'd seen Hannah shoot at Erculo's range as well as on the simulator in the shop basement. There was no doubt that the Lynx had hired somebody who could back him in a tight place.

Hannah was so exotic that her private life was a lot of the town's gossip. There weren't many facts available, though. Some people said she didn't like men, but others said she did—and didn't much care whether or not they were married.

It was real clear to anybody who watched her and the marshal together, though, that the Lynx wasn't getting anything that wasn't in a deputy marshal's normal job description.

Lincoln Feldshuh was at least sixty. He was fat and combed his hair carefully so he could pretend he hadn't already lost most of it. He must have slowed up some to leave Division 30 dueling and take the job of town marshal here when Big Ben Wallace offered it. The fact that the Lynx had survived fifteen years of arena competition—though he hadn't been a kid when he started—proved that he could slow down a lot and still be better than anybody he was likely to meet around Mannheim.

For a moment, I thought it was going to break right then. I worried about Erculo. I was going to dive off the other side of the tractor so I'd have the double thickness of the rig's armor between me and the shooting, but Erculo was in the wrecker's cab. It wasn't armored to survive the kind of crossfire that'd rip it.

Besides the police van's front turret—the rear blister with its laser-guided missile launcher wouldn't bear when the van was bow-on to the Spike-K crew—there was a launching trough along either flank of the vehicle. These could hold a variety of loads, but the Lynx usually carried a short-range bunker-buster with a hundred pound warhead in the left trough and seven folding-fin rockets with flechette warheads on the right.

The rockets had laser fuzes that spewed the flechettes out short of the target, forming a wall in the air. They were meant to riddle personnel and light vehicles at long range. I didn't know what they might do at point-blank like this on Stannard Kames' heavily armored CHIEF.

Most of the Spike-K crew were cowboys, not gunmen,

but they were a hard lot and all of them knew which end of
a gun the bang came out of. The turret on CHIEF's shelltop
mounted a high-velocity 30mm automatic with dual feed, so
that the gunner could switch from armor-piercing to high explosive, depending on the target. There was a wire-guided
antitank missile on either side of the turret besides.

There were three more six-wheeled pickups in the pack,
two of them flanking CHIEF in the front row. That pair
mounted a big recoilless and two pods of seven fourteen-
pound warhead rockets, plus the usual assortment of chassis
machine guns. The heavy in the back row, covering the caravan's rear, carried twin 20mm Gatlings that could swallow a
pickup's load of ammo in five seconds max. That'd be a *very*
bad five seconds to be down-range of the guns, though.

The remainder of the Spike-K pickups were working vehicles, not particularly formidable despite the number of extra
machine guns and automatic grenade launchers clamped to
the boxes for this operation and manned by tough-looking
cowboys. I'd seen a crew just like them cripple Big Ben Wallace, though, and there were sure enough heavy weapons in
this face-off to suit anybody who didn't figure to be in the
crossfire.

"Are you ready, boy?" Erculo demanded.

I couldn't imagine why he was so determined to get on
with a towing job when a major war was about to break out.
But he was, and I knew better than to argue when Erculo gave
an order.

"Pull away!" I shouted. Instead of climbing down, I
jumped off the far side of the tractor and hit the ground eight
feet below with my knees flexed.

The wrecker's powerful winch began to whine while I
was still in the air. The Lynx and Stannard Kames were

shouting threats at one another through roof speakers—both CHIEF and the police van were buttoned up, as was Big Ben's limo.

Ditsy—I hadn't noticed her before!—Ditsy was hanging out of the cherrypicker bucket of the TV truck, filming the whole scene and ad-libbing an explanatory voice-over. Just like the gypsy truckers' feeds, the signal was bounced to a comsat and back to K660's ground link at the station. If the next few minutes continued in the direction they were heading, Ditsy would have a clip on the national news, all right—but as exposed as she was in the bucket, she wouldn't be around to take a bow.

Under the tow truck's pull, the wrecked longnose heaved up on its side, then flopped back down on its wheels. The big tractor came to rest right across State 149, blocking the road and throwing an armored barrier between the two factions.

It struck me that Erculo saw more with his one eye than most guys did with two good ones.

Everybody relaxed. Much as the parties hated each other, I think they'd realized that they *all* were going to die in a point-blank knifefight like the one that had been brewing. Nobody could maneuver. Stray rounds and secondary explosions would have taken out half the population of the region besides.

Stannard Kames got out of his truck. He had to ease CHIEF forward a little to open the door. After a moment, the Lynx and Big Ben Wallace dismounted as well—Big Ben rolling down the ramp custom-built into his new Grenadier to accept his powered wheelchair. There was a sawed-off shotgun built into one of the chair's armrests, and Kames and the Lynx carried holster weapons; but the real danger of a holocaust had passed.

Stannard Kames was tall and gray and rangy. He had the complexion of weathered cowhide. From what I'd heard, the man himself was just about that tough too.

"I've seen the footage of this attack, Marshal," Kames said in a hoarse, harsh voice. By shifting to the side, he was able to see the Lynx over the wreck's fifth wheel, but he would have had to bend and squint beneath the chassis to glimpse Big Ben in the wheelchair.

The cattleman gestured toward the hole in the tractor's Spalltex windshield, centered on where the driver's chest had been. "This wasn't just a biker raid," he continued. "Some prime duelist fired *that* shot, and I guess we all know that your boss is the only man hereabouts to hire duelists!"

Big Ben spun his chair around the back of the tractor. "What's the matter, Kames?" he shouted. "D'ye think everybody ought to use home-grown thugs just because you do?"

"Sir," said the marshal in a low voice as he very deliberately walked between the wheelchair and the Spike-K guns, "I think it might be best if I handled this from here on out."

The Lynx looked Stannard Kames up and down in professional appraisal, as cool as if he didn't realize that his plump old body would catch the first blast if shooting started. He wore body armor, but nothing a human could carry would so much as slow the heavy weapons deployed here.

"Mr. Kames," he said, "we're all on the same side here. I sympathize with your loss—the crew, I mean. I've lost people a time or two, and I know how it made *me* feel."

Kames looked confused. I doubt he'd even known the names of the dead driver and gunner. The marshal praising him for a concern he hadn't shown did as much to defuse the tension as Erculo had when he rolled the barrier into place.

"As for it not being mere bike scum," continued the Lynx, "I agree with you. This was a professional operation. They had first-class shooter and a rig of their own to pack away the loot."

He thumbed toward the crumpled semi. "Your trailer's been stripped, not just picked over. But—"

The old man's face went blankly hard, the way I reckon it looked over his gunsights.

"—having your folks and mine blow each other to Hell won't do a thing to solve the real problem."

Kames grimaced, then made his decision. Instead of replying directly to the marshal, he called, "Erculo, hold the rig in your lockup. I'll be in touch with you to discuss salvage."

He turned and got back into CHIEF. Scraping and crunching like the world's worst parking-lot nightmare, the Spike-K pickups reversed and roared back down the road toward the ranch. They hadn't even bothered to carry away the bodies of the rig's crew.

I crawled under the tractor to release the drag lines before Erculo had to tell me. One of the hooks had slipped off the stanchion when the suspension flexed under the cab's weight, but the other was cramped in tight. I finally loosened it with my bootheel, on the last kick before I slid back out to get a hammer.

It was gritty and hot under the tractor. The projectile that hit the driver had been moving so fast that most of his chest had sprayed all over the interior of the cab. I'd gotten blood on my jeans when we lifted out the body, and it was beginning to spoil. I wasn't feeling real well, and I figured I'd shower at the shop before we came back for the gutted trailer.

The pearl-white sedan I'd seen go past earlier in the morning pulled up as I reappeared from under the tractor. Erculo had run the tow truck forward so that part of the road was clear, but the stranger didn't try to drive past.

I didn't recognize the make of car. It was smooth as an egg, with flexible skirts around the whole lower body down to the ground. It wasn't some sort of air-cushion special, though. I could see ordinary tires underneath where the lower edges of the skirt had been buffed away on rough roads.

The car didn't mount any obvious weaponry. Close-up like I was, I noticed a port just forward of the front door seam, but from the size and location I was pretty sure it was a smoke-bomb discharger rather than an offensive weapon. The back and rear-seat windows were polarized into shimmering blanks, like a limousine's, but it didn't seem like there was room enough for a millionaire to stretch out in privacy.

Nor did the driver look like anybody's chauffeur. He was a handsome man whose lips quirked a smile no deeper than the tan on his skin. His eyes flickered over everything without seeming to rest anywhere. When they touched me, I froze.

Lynx Feldshuh must have felt something similar. The marshal had been out of his vehicle since the Spike-K gang pulled away. Now he stepped back to the van's open side-door.

I almost missed the name of the stranger's car. It was in small print, true white against pearl white, on the frame above the side window: THE SQUARE DEAL.

The driver's door, a gullwing design hinged to the center of the roof, pivoted upward. The stranger got out and nodded pleasantly to me before he surveyed the crowd again.

He was a tall fellow and broad-shouldered. He wore a flat-crowned, broad-brimmed hat and a fringed serape of fine weave. The serape's pattern of rich colors came from a long way to the southwest.

A pair of chained silver conchos clasped the serape at his throat. There was room beneath its spreading folds to conceal anything from a derringer to a mortar, but he didn't look the sort who thought it took a big gun to be a big man.

He said in a clear, strong voice, "Good morning to you all. Mrs. Rachel Deal told me that I'd find her son Brian here. Might I speak to him, please?"

Billy Bristow began to hoot with laughter. Jack Terry blipped the klaxon on the roof of his car and shouted, "Hey, Deadeye! Your mommy's calling you!"

I went red and grabbed up the drag lines, pretending to be busy. Other people started laughing too.

The stranger turned slowly till he was facing me. The serape's fringe wove side-to-side with the motion. He was wearing a belt of shiny conchos like the ones in the clasp, and I didn't see a weapons holster at all.

"Excuse me, sir," the stranger said when he was sure I wasn't going to speak to him. "Would you be Mr. Brian Deal?"

I could see Ditsy in the cherrypicker, with her parabolic mike aimed right in my face. Terry hit the klaxon again, and one of his gang tried to wind up a siren that broke into a gurgle in the middle of the rising note.

Hannah Martin reacted to the noise by rotating the back turret of the police van to bear on the Pirates. Not really a threat, unless they didn't quiet down—which they did.

The only sound was the breeze through the scrub and the buzz of blood in my ears. I faced the stranger. "Who wants to know?" I demanded.

The stranger smiled, half humor, half in appraisal. "If you're Brian," he said in a mild voice, "then that's no way to greet your long-lost brother. I'm JC Deal."

CHAPTER 3

I heard the words, but they didn't touch me for a moment. It was like I was listening to a pair of strangers talk.

JC didn't expect an answer, though. He turned and called to Erculo, up in the tow truck's cab, "Sir? Erculo, is it not? I realize it's an imposition, but I'd like to carry Brian home to our mother. It'll be the first time the three of us have been together in twelve years."

"John—" I said and stopped.

I didn't know what to say. I didn't even know what to *call* my brother. He'd been John when he left, but I was a six-year-old kid and he was no older than I was now. The JC Deal standing in the middle of State 149 was still as much a stranger as he'd been when he stepped out of his gleaming car.

"Yes, all right," said Erculo. His face was wrinkled in a speculative frown, as if he were planning a particularly

29

complicated repair. "Hook up the tow lines and then go, boy."

The cherrypicker squeaked down to its platform. Ditsy hopped out of the bucket, carrying a hand-held camera. She didn't need to pan a battle scene, so she was going to do a close-up interview with JC Deal.

"But I want you back here in an hour to help me with the rest," Erculo resumed. In a milder voice, he added, "It's not the money I pay the boy, Mr. Deal. Alone, I can't handle a trailer so big, not even stripped to the struts as the gang left it."

While I scrambled to attach the first of the chain hooks, JC set the second one swiftly and expertly. People had gotten out of their cars again and edged closer, but nobody actually got in the way. To them, my brother was an unusual stranger—and when "unusual" survived in this world, it was dangerous.

Mom used the death benefit the Chicago courier company paid on Dad to move the three of us to Mannheim. She wanted a quiet place where we could live away from urban dangers that could smash *anybody* flat in an eyeblink.

The way a hijack team, equipped and organized like a small army, had taken out Dad.

Peace and quiet weren't what my brother was looking for. John—JC—had left home within a month of our coming here, so even folks who'd been in Mannheim twelve years ago weren't likely to remember him.

Besides, whatever Mrs. Deal's older boy had been when he left, it was different from the cat-quick man who'd returned in a car that gleamed like a pearl.

JC straightened and touched one of the conchos on his

belt. THE SQUARE DEAL's passenger-side door lifted like an owl flapping. "Hop in, boy," he said.

For the first time since JC pulled up, I thought about my clothes. "I can't get in like this, J-j—sir," I blurted. "I'm all over blood!"

"Get in," JC repeated, but it wasn't an offer anymore. "I've seen blood before, boy. So should you have, by now."

"Boy!" called Erculo. I looked up. Erculo tossed my grenade launcher to me from the wrecker cab with a stiff-armed motion, as if he were putting the shot.

I ducked quickly into THE SQUARE DEAL. The seats were firm and cool to the touch. The interior was upholstered in amber-colored wipe-clean plastic, rather than the leather I'd expected from the iridescent white body shell.

The driver's instrument package was simple: a video display to the right of the steering column combined the functions of many separate gauges. A console divided my seat from JC's. It was too high to be part of the drive train, so it had to conceal a centerline weapons installation. Nothing unusual there.

The sedan didn't have a back seat. Where that should have been was a huge purple-tinged drum, set vertically and shimmering like it was coated with oil.

"Admiring my flywheel, Brian?" JC asked with a chuckle. He touched a switch on the dashboard.

Ditsy forced her way through the crowd, holding out the camera as she called, "Mr. Deal? Mr. Deal?" She had to jump back to keep from being caught as the car doors closed. THE SQUARE DEAL didn't seem like the sort of vehicle that would have safety features to stall the doors before they pinched off a careless arm.

"Sir?" I asked.

"Touch it," JC said. "Carefully."

I reached out with one finger. The purple mass flicked me away. The drum was spinning at a high rate, but its surface was so smoothly featureless that only a quiver of light betrayed the movement to my eye.

"It's a way to store energy," JC explained, still smiling. "Also, a big drum of depleted uranium like that makes it real hard for unfriendly sorts to spoil our day from behind, not so?"

He laughed, not a particularly nice sound. "Hope you're not worried about a little low-level radiation, lad. It's not high on *my* list of dangers."

I nodded like I knew what JC was talking about. In a way I did, especially about the way the flywheel provided rear armor. I'd figure out the rest quick enough. Right then my brain was full of the fact that I had a brother again—and with wondering why.

Terry and the Pirates were moving. The reaper blades on I'M BAD's front fenders weren't serious weapons, but they sure shoved spectators back to the protection of their cars. "Hey, Deadeye!" Jack called with his head out the window. "Runnin' home to mommy?"

The Lynx watched from the open door of his van. What I saw in the old duelist's eyes made me shiver. *He* knew what was coming; better than I did, maybe better than Jack and his crew. The Lynx was interested, but it wasn't his business to interfere. He'd just watch.

I've seen blood before, boy. . . . JC knew what was coming, too.

JC pulled THE SQUARE DEAL into a tight turn at walking speed. We had a clear field because people were scurrying to get clear of the Pirates' lead cars. I'M BAD was coming up on our right; on the left was Little Boy Platt's CHINLESS WONDER with an overhanging ram plate and a pintle-mounted 20mm cannon—really too powerful for the chassis—manned by Davey Pringle, who lived on the dole and couldn't afford a car of his own.

"Buckle your harness, boy," JC ordered, checking the windows and both wing mirrors with tiny flicks of his eyes.

"It's buckled, sir," I said.

It didn't seem real, so I wasn't as scared as I knew I ought to be. I worked the action of my grenade launcher to chamber the first round. I wasn't carrying a bandolier of ammo, so I only had the three grenades in the magazine.

"Don't worry about that!" JC said contemptuously. "Can you use a targeting laser?"

I was starting to get angry—at JC, for treating me like a kid in what I figured were going to be the last couple minutes of my life.

"You bet," I said as I rotated over to me the goggles attached to the headliner by a telescoping boom. The left eyepiece was clear glass, so that I could see my surroundings normally through it. The right one provided a reflex image from the targeting head, and the dial on the side of the goggles rotated the mount with its superposed optical/laser lenses.

It took a lot of practice to operate a rangefinder with both eyes open simultaneously, but that was the only way you could both acquire and engage multiple targets *fast*. Erculo's simulator had given me more experience with that than most duelists had.

"*Not* before I tell you," my brother ordered. "And spot me drivers, just the drivers."

We'd continued crawling along 149 as though JC was waiting for the Pirates to drop into formation with us. I'M BAD and CHINLESS WONDER came alongside. I thought they might pull on ahead and give JC's forward-firing weapon a shot at one of the cars at least before the rest of the gang whomped us, but Jack Terry wasn't quite that stupid.

Jack leaned out again and hammered on my closed window with his fist. "C'mon Deadeye," he screamed. "Come and play, pussy!"

I kept my face set straight ahead, but I couldn't help blushing again. Out of the corner of my eye, I saw Jack's girlfriend pull down her spandex shorts and moon us from the back seat.

On the other side, Pringle pointed his long-barreled autocannon down so that the muzzle wavered close to JC's left ear. Platt revved CHINLESS WONDER to buzz and jingle the driveline fins.

JC opened his window a crack. "Sirs," he called. "I'm a stranger here. Surely you're not challenging me?"

"You bet your sweet ass we are!" Platt said. He cut his wheel to the right. His ram plate chipped THE SQUARE DEAL'S front fender and sent a solid shock through our armor.

"Going to send your mommy out to play, then, pussies?" Jack Terry shrieked.

The other four cars followed in two lines, bumper to bumper with the leaders. We'd finally eased past the civilian vehicles parked to view the hijacked rig.

JC rolled up his window. "D'ye know why people let themselves get into slanging matches with punks, boys?" he asked in a light, tight voice.

"No sir," I said.

"Neither do I," said my brother as his left little finger touched a wand on the control column and his foot stamped down on the accelerator.

I'd been right about the smoke dischargers forward of the door hinge, but I'd forgotten that even an ordinary smoke grenade makes a pretty good weapon when it's lobbed through a car's open window. The two grenades chunked out simultaneously, into Platt's lap and the back seat of I'M BAD.

JC's grenades were filled with white phosphorus. The Pirate cars mushroomed into dreadlock plumes of smoke that trailed from dazzling points. Willie Pete made a dense, white cloud that shielded anything behind it—but it would also burn through a man's flesh until the sparks fell to the ground beneath his thrashing body.

I didn't have time to appreciate that because THE SQUARE DEAL slammed me back in the seat cushions with acceleration like I'd never felt before in a four-wheeled vehicle. *Now* I knew what my brother meant about storing energy, because the flywheel screamed as its enormous rotational mass was braked to send a huge jolt of power to the wheels.

CHINLESS WONDER'S twenty mike-mike fired when Pringle clamped the trigger as he burned alive. That didn't matter to us because THE SQUARE DEAL was thirty feet down the highway and clear of the muzzle.

I spun the targeting head. The little rooftop mounting rotated on glass-smooth gimbals, giving me a right-eye view of the scene behind us. Recoil from the automatic cannon had flipped Platt's car, just like I figured it would. CHINLESS WONDER rolled off the road with boxed ammo popping like the 4th of July.

The next two Pirate cars were pulling around their burning leaders. I saw somebody jump out of I'M BAD, but flames wrapped the body so I couldn't tell whether it was Jack or his late girlfriend; 20mm ammunition exploded, tossing fragments high in the air.

I thought we were headed straight into town. Even without the flywheel's power boost, THE SQUARE DEAL was obviously faster than the Pirates' junkers. None of the survivors would push it, not after what had happened to their friends.

Instead, JC screamed, ''Target a driver and hang on!'' THE SQUARE DEAL hunkered down on her suspension as JC threw the car into a screaming turn that seemed to spin us in our own length.

I couldn't believe that forward momentum didn't flip us off the road—

But driving wasn't my business, targets were.

I clicked the stabilizer when the center dot in my right lens lay on Hank Mueller driving THE WAR HORSE. Hank was blasting away with the machine guns under his hood, and his cousin in the back was trying to aim the post-mounted anti-tank rocket that was probably the most dangerous weapon the Pirates had. Mostly, they couldn't afford effective heavy equipment and made do instead with whatever they thought looked good.

The stabilizer held the sight picture wherever the operator—me—aimed it, regardless of THE SQUARE DEAL's own motion. It was theoretically possible to stabilize a weapon, even one as big as a tank cannon, but the inertia involved kept that from being a practical proposition. I could follow THE WAR HORSE with the sight dot, though, and guide in what I thought would be a laser-homing missile that JC would launch.

AS THE SQUARE DEAL's smooth nose swung in the direction of THE WAR HORSE, the machine gun buried in the console between me and JC hammered. The whole car bucked. A gush of smoke hazed our windshield.

Beyond the smoke, Hank Mueller lurched backward from his seat and THE WAR HORSE spun out of control. JC had punched a pattern of holes tight enough to cover with my palm through the armored windshield, right where the driver was sitting.

Yellow flashes crackled against JC's side window. HEAVY METAL had gotten clear of I'M BAD and was raking us with incendiary bullets from the twin machine guns in its cupola.

That was maybe the worst threat, but DRAGON WAGON was right behind THE WAR HORSE when Hank Mueller flipped, so my sights were square on the Bristows' car. I toggled the designator button ON again, with the bright dot covering Billy as he cramped his wheel to line up the underslung recoilless rifle.

Another burst from our axial weapon shook THE SQUARE DEAL. Our bullets sparked on the top of DRAGON WAGON's hood and shattered the car's windshield. Ben Bristow leaped up from his loading position in the back seat. His face wore a startled expression. There were splotches of blood on his blue shirt where he'd been hit by bullets that must have drilled through his brother to get to him.

DRAGON WAGON collided with THE WAR HORSE. The shock of impact or Billy's dying reflex fired the one-oh-five. Backblast and a high-explosive anti-tank shell turned the joined wreckage into a single orange fireball.

JC turned *hard*, unbelievably hard. THE SQUARE DEAL spun on a dime while our flywheel screamed as it poured more power to the wheels. We tore west along State 149 again.

We couldn't outrun bullets, but our bootlegger turn and high acceleration threw off the guns that had caught us a moment before. HEAVY METAL's cupola didn't have a power traverse. The gunner, Vince Frawley or one of his farm-kid buddies, had to crank around the weight of armor and the twin machine guns with a handwheel. They couldn't track a target moving fast at an angle to wherever the guns were already pointing.

I centered the sight ring where HEAVY METAL's driver ought to be, because that was the order JC gave me, and this wasn't any time to argue about it. I wasn't sure it was going to work, though: Frawley had fitted thick shutters to the upper coaming of his windshield. They were locked down, now. That gave the driver only a narrow slit to see through, but two inches of opaque plating beside the clear Spalltex protected him.

"Hang—" JC shouted.

Something blew up like the wrath of God on the rear of THE SQUARE DEAL. The shock flung me back in my seat. The car filled with the sweetish, waxy stink of explosive residues. We fishtailed bad enough that I thought JC had lost control.

He hadn't. THE SQUARE DEAL made another of her patented turns, swinging her nose to bear on the remaining targets. Our tires shrieked like four damned souls, but they held the road.

I refocused the laser sight. HEAVY METAL's forward motion had pulled the car half a length out of the proper picture while I bounced against my restraints and thought I was about to die. As I clicked the dot live, our centerline gun ripped and bucked. The explosion a moment before must have loosened the console's soundproofing panels, because the noise was deafeningly loud and the bitter smell of powder gases made me cough.

The target's driver-side shutter sparkled in the long burst that JC poured into it. I couldn't tell whether or not our shots were penetrating the thick armor, but after three seconds the hinged plate fell away from the windshield.

HEAVY METAL continued to roll forward, but smoke

poured out of cracks in the body panels. The cupola machine guns swung skyward. The gunner was clinging to the grips as his body slid to the floor of the riddled vehicle.

There was one Pirate vehicle left. I'd have said it was a joke—except that this was the one that had hit THE SQUARE DEAL a moment before, and *that* knock sure wasn't funny.

Tink Weatherspoon and his sister, a kid who padded her bra with rags whenever she thought her father wasn't within range to swing his belt, had hung armor plating on an ancient Ford-Ferguson farm tractor. Flat out, it could maybe run as fast as I could, and it looked about as silly as a rabbit with horns.

They'd welded a 75mm recoilless rifle to the top of the cab. I didn't think they could hit anything with it, since they'd made their own iron sights to replace the smashed laser gear the gun had had in its original truck-turret installation.

They'd hit us once, though. I figured it was God's mercy to me and JC that to reload the rifle on its jury-rigged mount, Sis Weatherspoon had to stand on the back edge of the driver's seat and cling to the roof coaming with her free hand. One shot was all they got.

They knew that too. Even before I could rotate my sight onto the tractor, Tink and Sis both jumped out of the open back of the cab. They ran toward the scrub, pumping their arms like wind-up toys. The tractor continued to trundle up the road toward us.

JC slowed THE SQUARE DEAL to a crawl and began to turn. I pivoted the sighting goggles back into their standby position against the headliner. When I grinned at my brother, I could see in the corner of my eye that the flywheel was spinning noticeably slower than before.

"We did—" I started to say.

"I thought," JC said in a cold snarl that slapped me harder than a shout would have done, "that I told you to target drivers, *boy*."

"But I did!" I said.

JC squeezed the trigger ring on the inner surface of the steering wheel. He was still looking at me, not out the front of the car. Our gun fired. Milkweed stems a hundred yards beyond the Weatherspoons quivered from bullets that had to pass through the kids to get there. Both of them fell down.

"Next time," JC grated, "don't quit till I tell you the job's done."

I blinked and stared out the windshield instead of toward my brother. Several vehicles had started toward us when they thought the fight was over. The fresh burst of gunfire froze all of them again except for the TV truck.

To my amazement, Tink Weatherspoon got to his feet again and resumed a shambling run. He was still moving despite being hit by a gun that had perforated heavy armor.

JC thumbed a switch on the left spoke of the steering wheel. A hidden lamp projected an orange sighting circle onto the windshield in front of him.

"SLAP rounds aren't great for anti-personnel," he said as he peered deliberately through the reflector sight, "but—"

His right index finger tapped the trigger. The gun between us *crack*ed once, violently. Tink threw up his hands and flopped forward again.

"—they'll do in a pinch," JC concluded. He tightened his turn, running onto the shoulder and back, and accelerated gradually when THE SQUARE DEAL was headed west again.

Behind us, the fire brewing within HEAVY METAL reached a critical point. The car ruptured with a crash and a sullen fireball. A column of black smoke reached hundreds of feet into the sky and flattened into a mushroom top.

"Ma'll be wondering what's taking me so long," my brother muttered.

Out of the smoke rained fragments of plating; the entire cupola, tumbling over and over; and, I think, a human arm.

CHAPTER 4

"You handled the sight well, Brian," JC said mildly. He drove like he was part of the car, making minimal corrections to the wheel.

I swallowed. "Thank you, sir," I said without looking at him. "I practice a lot."

"First time you've been in the real thing, though, wasn't it?"

THE SQUARE DEAL had the stiff ride required for crisp handling. At our present moderate speed, I was more aware of the weight of armor—and the flywheel—than I had been during the ten-tenths stress of the firefight, when the power-plant was at full output.

"Yessir," I said. "It was."

"Brian," my brother said, "if you'll try to remember not to call me 'sir,' I'll try not to call you 'boy.' "

I turned. JC was looking at me, smiling slightly. "Okay, JC," I said. "I—I'm a little shook, is all."

JC swerved to avoid a pothole that would have swallowed a front wheel. He'd seen it out of the corner of his eye, but it made him—or allowed him—to face front again. "Once I start, I only know one way to go, Brian," he said. "That's all the way to the end. If you think I'm hard, I'm sorry . . . but it's a hard world out there, and—"

He turned his head and waited until I met his eyes.

"—and I've found that you don't have to give a warning but once, so long as you tell people the right way the first time."

I couldn't think of anything I wanted to say, so I just nodded.

JC went back to his driving. "You're a slick operator with the sight," he said toward the windshield. "Six on one would have been a real problem if you hadn't been so good."

"I don't see how you shot like that and drove at the same time," I said, glad for the change of subject. "I figured I'd be guiding in missiles, but you were just using regular bullets, weren't you?"

JC nodded, grinning. "SLAP rounds, yeah; saboted light armor-piercing. I'm loaded with tungsten penetrators now, but I run depleted uranium when I can find it. If you can keep the dispersion low, a long burst of D.U. 'll peck through about any armor you can mount on four wheels. Six wheels, if it comes to that, though I wouldn't really want to try conclusions head-on with your sheriff, there. Lynx Feldshuh, isn't he?"

"You know the Lynx, then?" I said in surprise. "He's the town marshal here, yeah."

"I've seen him in the arena," JC said. "Maybe a time

or two out of it. Didn't really figure to meet him wearing a badge, but I reckon we'll cross that bridge when we come to it."

There wasn't any emotion in his voice. His words were as smooth and flat as the console covering THE SQUARE DEAL's weapon.

JC cleared his throat and continued, "As for driving and shooting—I just drove. In a manner of speaking, *you* did all the shooting, Brian. All save the last, I mean."

"Me?"

Because of the flywheel, we couldn't look straight out the back of THE SQUARE DEAL. JC's eyes kept flicking from one wing mirror to the other. I edged forward so that I could see what was behind us in the mirror on my side.

"Oh," I said. "That's Ditsy Wallace from the TV station. She's, well, she's a real hotdog on a story. She'll want to interview you for, for . . ."

I leaned back in my seat again. A shootout like *that* one could make the national news. And I'd been right in the middle of it.

"Well, she'll have to wait till we've had family time," JC said. He glanced over at me. "Friend of yours, is she?"

"Sometimes," I said. "Yeah, I think so."

JC chuckled for a moment. "About shooting, then," he went on. "The gun—"

He patted the console.

"—is on an axial mount, which is the *only* damned way you can hit anything when you're moving fast."

With a snort, he added, "A thing that kids like back there don't live long enough to learn. Anyhow, I turn the car with the gun on autotrip—"

JC's right index finger indicated but did not touch a toggle switch on the steering wheel spoke.

"—and the gun fires when it bears on the target you've highlighted. The gun's default impact is forty inches at a hundred yards, but the mount's got two degrees of elevation and traverse. Since the gun's slaved to the laser sight, that keeps the dispersion *way* down. All I need to do is steer in the direction of the vector arrow on my windshield."

JC tapped the armored glass, though no indicator was reflected there at the moment. He smiled. "Good target selection, Brian," he added. "And you're fast as well as steady, which maybe saved our lives. Thanks, brother."

I licked my lips. It seemed simple the way JC explained it, but it was his brutal quickness, slamming THE SQUARE DEAL in tight figure-eights to engage and disengage, that had reduced the Pirates to blazing junk in a matter of minutes.

And I knew that JC could have done the job without me. I'd seen the way his offhand burst cut down the Weatherspoons. There wasn't the least doubt that my brother's reflector sight and Mark I eyeball would have settled a gang of farm kids in junkers. He didn't need laser targeting.

"I understand the acceleration," I said carefully, "with the flywheel coupled to the drive train. But I don't see how you turned us like that. I didn't think *anything* could turn that tight."

Except I *had* seen another sedan reverse direction on a dime, just the night before. Before it shot the driver of the Spike-K rig as expertly as my brother had dropped Tink Weatherspoon.

JC laughed merrily. "Oh, that's a little trick of the old girl's," he said, patting the dashboard. "You noticed our skirts?"

"Yes s—I mean, yes, JC," I said. "But an air cushion doesn't help turning, you've got no traction at all!"

"It's not a cushion, Brian," JC explained. "I'm not blowing air into it, I'm sucking it out when I want to turn tight. The down-force from the partial vacuum glues us right to the road—"

He laughed again. "*If* the road surface is fairly firm— don't try it on loose gravel. And *don't* try it when somebody's shot your skirt into a colander. The skirt's not armored, you know, just stiffened rubber. I made that mistake once and damn near got killed, except the way I went hopping around the highway threw off the blister gunner's aim. *Not* one of my better efforts."

JC's voice lilted, and he shook his head as though it was just a joke he was telling. But I saw his eyes, and there was no humor in them.

We'd reached Mannheim; not that the town was much to reach. A few heads poked out of windows. The few stay-at-homes had been alerted by CB radio about what happened at the wreck site.

We drove past Erculo's shop and K660 across the highway from it. You could say that Big Ben had most of Mannheim nailed down. Security Warehouse, which Wallace owned, was south of town on State 149. Mannheim had only one real cross street, Liberty, and Big Ben had built his new house—fortified like an arsenal—on the east end of it.

Wallace's Hardware and the Mannheim Bank were on corners of Liberty and State 149, naturally. About the only thing Big Ben lacked was the west end, where Mom and I lived. I hadn't really thought of it that way until I rode through Mannheim beside my brother.

Mom stood in front of the little house, with her hands

pressed tightly together like she was praying. JC pulled in smoothly to the power connection. I don't think it had been used in the twelve years since he left town. He touched a dashboard switch and the gullwing doors lifted.

I felt stiff as I got out. I'd been so tense during the firefight that I must have strained muscles just by them pulling against each other.

JC moved like a cat, smooth and perfectly in balance. He never seemed to be in a hurry, but his motions were always complete before you quite realized he started to do something. He spread his arms, lifting the serape and causing the concho belt to gleam in the sunlight.

The fresh air was unexpectedly good. Despite THE SQUARE DEAL's climate control, the car's interior smelled of powder smoke and the blood stiffening on my clothes.

Mom threw herself against JC's chest. She didn't seem to notice that I existed. "Oh, John," she murmured. "You've been fighting. I knew you had."

JC chuckled. "Now, Ma," he said, "there wasn't anything to it. You know how dogs all think they've got to snap at a stranger before they let him settle in. Nothing more than that."

I stared at THE SQUARE DEAL. The left side was pocked by dozens of bullets from when HEAVY METAL had raked us with its cupola guns. On the right side—my side—were a couple bigger craters; I could fit my clenched fist into them. Jacket metal from the shells gave the dents a brassy sheen. Something heavy, at least a cal fifty, had hit us square and come within an ace of penetrating.

I thought back, trying to remember the impacts, but I couldn't. The firefight was a blur of shocks and flashes, all viewed through the red sheen of my targeting laser.

I walked to the back of the car. THE SQUARE DEAL's trunk lid was dished in and blackened where the 75mm shell had hit us.

JC looked at me over the top of the car, still holding Mom. "Just as well they were using HE Common instead of anti-tank, isn't it, brother? You know, I'm not sorry that pair won't be bothering us again."

The TV truck pulled up in the street in front of the house. Most of the folks in town seemed to be following Ditsy and her driver.

"I gotta go wash and change," I mumbled as I broke for the door to the house.

JC touched a concho on his belt. THE SQUARE DEAL's doors sighed closed. "I think it's time for us all to go in," my brother said coolly. "I don't care to give shows—unless I'm being paid for it."

CHAPTER 5

I showered as quick as I could, but I didn't guess till I got started how much I needed to clean off me. Especially from my hair. I kneaded my scalp for some minutes under the spray before I stopped feeling half-dried gumminess beneath my fingertips.

The smell of my work clothes hit me fresh when I stepped out of the shower. I tossed them into the shower stall and pulled the curtain. I'd deal with them later. Maybe the clothes could be washed, but right now burning them seemed the better idea.

The trucker's bloody death had been none of my doing. But I'd helped to do the same to maybe a dozen of—I won't say my friends, but kids I'd grown up with.

I put on a clean set of overalls and went out to join Mom and JC.

Mom bustled in the kitchen, talking twenty to the dozen

as she plucked one of the chickens from the pen out back. We eat pretty good here on the prairies. Not fancy, maybe, but beef is cheap and most everybody keeps their own poultry, chickens or rabbits, for Sunday dinner.

Sunday'd come early this week to the Deal household.

JC sat in the living room. He'd moved a chair to the corner of the room instead of sitting on the couch where there'd be glass behind him; but the blinds were open, and he watched out the front window through the reflection in the mirror over the TV.

JC nodded toward the window when he saw me. "You'd think more folks'd have homes to go to," he said with a smile that didn't go deeper than the skin of his lips.

I walked over to the window. Nigh the whole town was in the road outside, all right, just like they'd been at the wreck site a couple hours before. The truck from K660 was parked square in front. Ditsy was beside it holding a minicam while her driver crouched up in the bucket with the big camera.

Nobody had crossed what they figured was our property line, the walkway I'd graveled out toward the road and fringed with bigger rocks. I hadn't followed any survey or the like. I had some time one summer and built the walk for pretty till I got tired. Heck, Mom and I never used the front door anyhow.

Right now, folks were treating the street end of the walk like everything closer to the house had mines and guard dogs waiting. When they saw me at the window, they whispered and pointed. Ditsy even aimed her camera and began mouthing a voice-over to the film.

"I was wondering, Brian," JC said easily. "Do any of the people out there happen to be kin of the lot who jumped us on the highway?"

"Kin?" I said, squinting. "Well, there's Ella Romaine, her sister married Joe Terry, that's Jack's dad. And—"

I realized what my brother was really asking. "Oh," I said. "Look, JC, it's not like that. In Mannheim, we're . . . I mean, we're not gunmen. I reckon Luke and Millie Weatherspoon, they're going to be pretty broke up. Maybe some of the other parents, too. But nobody's going to come looking for you."

"Oh dear, ought I to use cream cheese or milk in the frosting?" Mom chattered from the kitchen. "John, you choose, I'm just too flustered to know which to use for a carrot cake!"

"Either'll do fine, Ma," JC said through his cold smile. "There's not a soul I met all the places I've been whose cooking was a patch on yours."

I could see the mockery in his eyes as he spoke; and I noticed that JC hadn't warned *me* when he thought there might be a bullet coming through the window. Maybe that was why I said, "Not Terry and the Pirates neither, if it comes to that. They'd drive around after chores or because it was something to do between dole checks, and maybe they'd scare a tourist or two. But they just wanted to feel big in a town where *no* damn thing's more than penny ante."

"Then they should've been more picky about which tourist they tried to scare," JC said with no emotion. His eyes studied the mirror, not me.

I could hear the boom of an amplified voice, but with the door and windows closed I couldn't make out the words. Two parked cars moved back out onto Liberty Street. The police van pulled up in their place, just ahead of the TV truck.

"I thought the local law would be paying me a visit after this morning," JC said mildly. "Well, no rest for the weary."

He got to his feet, took his brilliantly colored serape from the coat rack, and put on his hat. "I guess I can handle this myself, Brian."

"I'm coming," I said. My grenade launcher was in the kitchen, by the side door. I ducked past Mom to get it—and the bandolier I didn't usually bother to carry.

"What's going on?" she demanded, shocked out of her chatter about the meal. "John?"

"Nothing to worry about, Ma," JC said. "No problem at all, just a gentleman who wants to chat with me."

He hooked the silver clasp at his throat. The serape covered his hands and hid the fact he wasn't carrying any serious weapons.

Though I shouldn't say that, now that I'd seen what JC could make his conchoed belt do.

"I'm coming with you," Mom said firmly.

"Whatever you like," JC agreed with his mocking grin. He opened the front door and led us out. I walked to his left and a half-step behind. Mom was on JC's other side. The gravy ladle she carried made me feel a right fool with my grenade launcher and the belt of reloads.

Lynx Feldshuh walked deliberately toward the house, while it must be a hundred people watched—from their cars, or ready to duck behind them.

The Lynx knew better—or he wouldn't be sauntering up on foot. The old man wore a big-bore pistol on his right hip, but he put that on with his pants in the morning. It didn't mean trouble.

The police van was parked broadside to the house with its turrets trained fore-and-aft. That was only common sense, seeings as the Lynx would be between us and the weapons if shooting started.

The van's side door was open. Hannah Martin lounged

in it, looking sleek and relaxed—in the way a cat relaxes with an eye half-turned toward a mouse hole. Her leather slacks fit like she'd shrunk them on, and she'd shaken her hair loose in public for the first time since she'd come to town.

On the breeze, I could smell a faint tinge of smoke from THE SQUARE DEAL'S gun.

JC paused and stood arms akimbo, six feet from Feldshuh. He said, "This is twice in a day, Marshal. I don't know that it's an honor to see the law so often."

"You know, Deal," the Lynx said, "I don't need to see so much of you, neither. Except your back. I'd admire to see your back leaving Mannheim and not showing up again."

"If you've said your piece," JC replied, "then get off my property until the law gives you a reason—which it never will."

From the words you might think he was shouting, but he didn't raise his voice a bit. The syllables were soft and clipped, like shells being shucked through the action of a shotgun.

"Mannheim's a quiet little place, Deal," the marshal said a good bit louder. "We don't need duelists, and we don't want them! Why don't you get back where you belong?"

JC laughed like a crow calling, loud and harsh. "Well, you could've fooled *me*, old man. I thought you were that Lynx Feldshuh who was on the Northwestern Circuit for a coon's age—till he got fat and slow! Not so?"

"This isn't an arena, Deal," the Lynx said softly. "This is Mannheim, and—"

"Then let's look at just what *did* happen this morning, Lynx," JC broke in. "First off, I was challenged. You could maybe have headed the fight off, but you didn't choose to do that thing. Second, Marshal—there was six of them, or did that slip your mind?"

"They were kids!" snapped the Lynx. "Ben Bristow had just turned fourteen!"

"Well . . . ," said JC in a voice that dragged like chalk on a blackboard. "I don't reckon his folks need worry about a party next year, do they?"

For the least moment, I thought the marshal was going to draw—and I was going to see if I could poke my grenade launcher in his belly before he got the pistol clear, which I doubted. Then Hannah Martin chuckled from the door of the van.

JC stepped to the side and walked around the Lynx, delicately as a matador in the bullring. He unlatched the serape and swung it off with a quick movement that put a flow of vivid cloth between him and the marshal without seeming to be anything but chance motion.

"We haven't met, milady," JC said as he stepped toward the van. He kept the serape moving in circles as he walked, switching it from one hand to the other. The brilliant dyes were common to both sides of the weave, but the clasp's silver conchos blazed or dimmed as the serape moved.

"Haven't we?" Hannah asked in a throaty voice. "Seems I've met your type before, at least."

"Am I a type, then?" JC said with a chuckle. "Well, perhaps I am. And being the kindly type I am, I wouldn't want you to be cold, so—"

He twirled the serape the last arm's length toward Hannah and let it go.

"—why don't you take this to keep you warm?"

"What d'ye think you're playing at, Deal?" the Lynx snarled.

Hannah caught the serape one-handed—her left, not her gun hand—and smoothed the cloth to her bare bosom for a moment. "This is the only way you figure to keep me warm, then, fella?'' she asked, like she and my brother were alone in a bedroom.

"You're a big girl," JC said in the same kind of voice. "I reckon that's up to you."

"Lynx," I whispered as I raised the grenade launcher. "Don't do it." My grenade wouldn't arm if fired at so short a distance, but the smack it gave him would end matters right quick.

"Lincoln Feldshuh!" Mom cried. "Just get out of here now and stop harassing my boy! Where are you when a body can't walk from her house to the store without being mocked by young pipsqueaks?"

The Lynx glanced around. His face was livid. I'd spoken when I saw the veins standing out on his neck.

Mom shook the spoon in the marshal's face.

"Get us moving!" the Lynx ordered in a thick voice as he stumbled toward the van. JC stepped aside as neatly as he had done before.

Hannah Martin smiled toward my brother and slid back into the driver's seat before her boss reached the vehicle. She wasn't wearing the serape, but she folded it across her lap with her left hand.

The Lynx slammed shut the door of the van as soon as he was inside, but his voice bellowed an angry syllable toward his deputy before the latch caught. The van pulled out sedately, despite demands to "Put your foot in it, woman!" muted by the armor.

JC chuckled.

Erculo's motorcycle pulled into a small fraction of the spot the police vehicle had just vacated. I hadn't noticed Erculo's approach; but then, I hadn't noticed much for the last few moments except my aiming point on the back of Lynx Feldshuh's head.

"Mom, ah . . ." I said. "JC. I gotta go now. There's the semi to—"

I stopped. Mom was hugging JC and neither of them seemed to know I was alive. A hundred faces stared at us from the road: my neighbors, but I'd never seen them like this. It was like watching a shoal of carp gaping from muddy water, greedy for any tidbit you might throw.

Erculo walked toward us, lifting off his helmet as he came. He threw one disgusted glance over his shoulder at the spectators, so it wasn't just me. Ditsy fell into step behind him, advancing with the minicam. I didn't know how I felt about that.

Erculo's bike was stripped to the bare essentials. Its 21-inch wheels and knobby tires weren't out of place on our local roads, given the level of maintenance, and they permitted him to ride out into the hills alone when he chose to. I don't know that you'd say those rides were Erculo's recreation, but they were about the only thing he did except work on cars.

The bike had neither armor nor a weapon. I guess Erculo was trying to prove something or apologize for something. I didn't want to know what.

"I'm with you now, Erculo," I said. "Sorry I—"

"No, no," Erculo said with a quick wave of his helmet. He'd taken time to change at the shop into the full leathers and high boots that he invariably wore aboard the motorcycle. "Brian, you take the rest of the day off. The trailer, it isn't going anywhere. It will keep till we get to it."

"I can—" I began.

"No," said Erculo, "you can't. It hasn't hit you yet, but I don't want you handling power tools when it does."

"Mr. JC Deal," Ditsy interrupted in a bright voice as

56

she thrust the minicam toward my brother's face. "Can you give us a statement about the fight, sir?"

"Fight?" repeated JC. He gave Mom an additional squeeze and released her. "No, I don't think I can. We're rather busy right now. We were just getting dinner on the table."

Erculo peered closely at THE SQUARE DEAL. He measured the depth of the pocks in the side paneling with his index finger, though I noticed that he didn't quite touch the depressed surface; then he walked around to the back.

"Well, sir," Ditsy continued. My brother's grin brought spots of color to her cheeks, but she wasn't going to let that affect her delivery. "Can you tell our viewers what name you campaigned under on the circuits?"

"Little girl . . . ," JC said. "*If* I had a war name, I'd have taken it to get my private life private. Wouldn't I? Now you'll have to excuse us."

He stared pointedly at her feet, halfway up our walk.

"That was JC Deal, ladies and gentlemen," Ditsy continued with brittle cheerfulness, "winner in this morning's amazing one-against-six duel on State Highway 149 north of Mannheim, here in the Central Prairies. Mr. Brian Deal, what were you thinking when you accompanied your brother in this epic undertaking?"

"Ditsy," I whispered, "don't *do* this." I turned my back.

"Come along, Brian," Mom called sharply to me. She and JC were walking toward the house.

"Mr. Deal," said Erculo as he turned from THE SQUARE DEAL. "You will want repairs made to your car. It would be an honor to me to perform them. We see very few Tempest Motors vehicles in this part of the country."

JC faced around. His smile looked real, for the first time since I'd seen him. "You recognize her, then?"

A vehicle revved in the road. The TV truck pulled out. Ditsy was driving with her face set like a concrete block. The regular driver was still up in the bucket, clinging desperately and protesting through the interphone link.

Erculo nodded. "A Komet, is she not? A fine vehicle, a very fine vehicle."

"Actually, she's a Kormoran," JC explained. "Smaller by three inches of width and six in the wheelbase—but you've got to see them together before you can tell the difference. What—"

JC's tone changed. He was coolly appraising again. "What sort of work do you think she'll require, sir?" he continued.

Erculo nodded crisply. "The window, replacement for safety's sake. We could stress test it and it might pass, but that's a false economy. The side panels, buff and fill the small dents—"

My brother was nodding in pleased agreement.

"—they should be fine. The two large dents, buff, plug, and fill—unless the electroflux shows fractures beneath the twentieth lamina, in which case I'd want to replace. I don't think so, but the electroflux will show."

"And the rear panel?" JC asked.

Erculo shrugged. "Replace it, of course. I could machine a piece of armor from billet that would serve your practical purposes, but—I assume you would rather have the Tempest Motors part? Shipping from Long Island will take at least a week."

JC nodded.

"And the touch-up paint, that will have to come from Tempest Motors also," Erculo concluded.

"Very good," my brother said. "I'll bring the old girl in some time tomorrow." He reached into the breast pocket of his shirt. "I'll give you my account number, so you can start ordering—"

Erculo waggled his helmet again. "That won't be necessary, Mr. Deal," he said. "You will pay when you're satisfied with my work. As I said, this is an honor."

He nodded and stamped back to his motorcycle.

JC faced the crowd. "Show's over, folks," he called in a loud voice. "Nothing more to see here. I'd advise you all to get back to your affairs, because my brother and I, we might be registering weapons in the front yard in about ten minutes' time. Understood?"

He smiled. Anybody who didn't understand the words must have caught the hint from that wolfish expression, because the cars parked all along Liberty Street started up like somebody'd waved a flag.

"Come along, Brian," JC said quietly. "We got dinner to eat."

JC got his old room back. That put me out on the couch. It didn't matter a whole lot, because I couldn't sleep anyway. Every time my eyes closed, I saw blood and the dead faces of kids I'd known for a dozen years.

About midnight, JC went out again. He and Mom talked in the kitchen. Argued, I should say; I couldn't catch Mom's words, but the tearful cadences of her voice wavered up and down. At last JC said, "I'm a big boy now, Ma," and let the side door clap shut behind him.

I watched through the front window as THE SQUARE DEAL ghosted off into the night. In the kitchen, Mom cried.

CHAPTER 6

A ten-wheel flatbed with a 20mm Gatling in the cab turret rumbled down State 149 early the next morning. Erculo and I glanced up to identify the vehicle as the delivery truck from the Davidson and Sheen depot in Chalybeate Springs, then went back to our inventory of the wrecked tractor. The D & S flatbed was a fixture ever since Big Ben Wallace began stocking his store and warehouse through the new firm two months before.

Because we ignored the familiar truck, we missed THE SQUARE DEAL tucked in behind it until JC pulled into the lot. His door lifted.

"Good morning, gentlemen," JC called as he got out. He stretched, a movement that emphasized his lithe body and broad shoulders. Sunlight scattered from his belt.

JC looked tired, but good tired. The way he grinned at us made me think of the look Hannah Martin gave him in front of the house the past afternoon. "You've been busy," he added.

Erculo had been busy, not me. He'd towed the wrecks from the gunfight into his lockup. There hadn't been enough of HEAVY METAL to bother with after the brew-up; DRAGON WAGON and THE WAR HORSE had been dollied in together, what was left of them.

Tink and Sis Weatherspoon's undamaged tractor was in the lockup. I'd seen the kids' parents viewing the hijacked rig before the gunfight. They could've claimed the vehicle right there, but I guess they didn't want to see it again.

Neither did I, particularly.

I was glad Erculo hadn't asked me to tow in the Pirates' cars. I guess if I could help with the killing, I could help clean up the mess afterwards—but I sure didn't want to.

Either one, come to think.

"There's nothing that can't wait for your car, sir," Erculo said formally. "If you'll drive into the diagnostic bay, please?"

JC waved to THE SQUARE DEAL's open door. "You know where you want her," he said. "Go ahead."

As Erculo eased the car into the bay, my brother walked over to me. "Doing all right, Brian?" he asked.

"I'm keeping it between the ditches," I said. I wiped my hands on a shop rag before I took out the tools we were going to need on THE SQUARE DEAL. "We ought to have you fixed up in two hours max. What we can do this pass, I mean."

Cars pulled up in front of the shop like magic, about a dozen of them. There wasn't much going on around Mannheim. Mostly folks on the dole hung out at Wallace's Hardware and watched the big-screen TV, but there were usually some idlers around the shop too.

Half the time it would have been Terry and the Pirates, for all Erculo made it clear he didn't have any use for them. That was one problem violence had settled, no mistake. I'd have preferred the punks' gibes to the way my belly flipped when I glanced through the chain-link fence of the lockup, though.

JC and his car were the hottest show in town, now. I don't know how folks had learned THE SQUARE DEAL was back. Folks piled out of their cars and stood around me and my brother in a half-circle like they expected us to perform.

I guess what shook me most was when Joe Reith—looking sidelong at my brother—said to me, "Ah, Deadeye? I been thinkin' about adding a mine-drop package to my truck. I wonder, d'ye think they'd be clearance problems if'n we mounted it under the back?"

First, Joe Reith was fond of telling the world that his mongrel dog was smarter than the Deal boy.

Second, what Joe's pickup needed wasn't a mine-dropper but to be jacked up and have a new truck rolled in beneath it. If he ever got around to firing the machine gun mounted under his hood, the whole body would shake apart like a bomb went off.

Third—Joe Reith called me "Deadeye" as if he meant it.

The world had changed a lot since the morning before.

"Sorry, Mr. Reith," I said. "I've got work to do now."

I stepped into the bay, carrying my gear. I added over my shoulder, "I'm sure we'd be happy to discuss the modification soon as we've got a minute, though."

It felt good. It felt *real* good.

Erculo and I checked the pads twice before we clamped them on THE SQUARE DEAL and lifted the car on the three-axis rack. I hooked the electrodes to each body panel in turn while Erculo watched the screen. The electroflux unit's printer would give us hard copy, but Erculo liked to eyeball the data as it appeared.

THE SQUARE DEAL wasn't very big, but she was built like an anvil. Her armor was half again as thick at every point as I'd expected it to be. I'd figured the big dents on the left side came from a cal fifty. When I saw the door panels were four-inch instead of the three I'd guessed *max*, it seemed more likely that we'd been hit by a 20mm cannon. Maybe we'd been in the wrong place when I'M BAD's Gatling cooked off a few rounds.

Erculo watched in delight as I set the electrodes, working methodically from one panel to the next. The electroflux unit induced a minuscule charge in a piece of material. Stresses within the piece tested appeared as color codings on the phosphor screen.

Normally, even a piece of armor plate without battle damage showed rainbow striations caused during forming and attachment. Panels on THE SQUARE DEAL were a quiescent gray except where bullets pocked them green or occasionally yellow. The trunk panel where the 75mm shell hit verged into the orange. A proper heat-treatment would reduce the stresses to cold blue, but many laminae were penetrated and the panel would still be bowed.

"Tempest Motors builds very few cars, boy," Erculo said, watching the screen with his back to me. "But they build them well. A work of art, each one."

The last piece I checked was the skirt. The lower edge was worn a fiery orange, especially beneath the rear quarter-panels where the car had dug in during JC's 180° turns. The skirt hadn't taken any bullets during the fight with the Pirates.

There were no patches from previous damage either. I moved the electrodes and checked again, remembering JC's comment about losing control when his skirts were shot up.

"Nothing unexpected," Erculo said with satisfaction as he switched off the screen. "No frame damage whatever. So."

He considered the task, his lips moving silently. "I'll take care of the back armor, you buff the sides. Start with the deep holes. I'll fill them while you're popping back the rest."

We got down to business. I'd feared that THE SQUARE DEAL's thick armor would make her as tough as a truck cab to work on. Because she was car-sized, though, our three-axis rack lifted and rotated her into whatever position made the job easiest.

Made Erculo's job easy, anyhow. When he needed to bank the car 90°, left side down, to remove the rear panel, he did just that. I lay on my back and continued buffing away the film of bullet-core that had plated across the armor while the rest of the projectile splashed away.

The idlers drifted in and out of the bay, watching and kibitzing. Reith and Art Pecek, another dole-rat, crowded a bit too close. Erculo let the welding head throw an "accidental" arc that sprayed molten plastic across their shoes. That backed them off.

The pack of spectators spent a lot of time around the lockup, oohing and ahing over the Pirates' vehicles. "Could've heard Platt sizzle from here to Hoboken!" I heard somebody say. "He had a hot time of it, no mistake."

There was usually a little group standing near JC in the shade of the awning out front. Waiting for him to speak, I reckon. JC sipped a soda and smiled and didn't let on he knew there was another soul in fifty miles. It was a game for him. Harmless enough, but the way he used Hannah Martin to bait the Lynx was a game too. That one could've gotten somebody killed.

And the Pirates . . . they'd brought it on theirselves, but for my brother that had been just a game. Sort of like dropping rocks off a bridge and seeing how many frogs you could squash.

The delivery truck headed back north, highballing with the bed empty of the crates it had carried to Big Ben's warehouse. Chalybeate Springs had been just about a ghost town until Davidson and Sheen moved in and built a freight terminal. Ditsy'd told me they were a chain with a number of bases throughout the Midwest. When they came to this area, their slogan was, "You don't know who we are, so we're out to convince you with low prices and high quality."

I guess they'd done all right, at least on price, because Big Ben had pretty well switched over to Davidson and Sheen as a supplier in the past two months. I hadn't noticed that *his* retail prices came down any, though.

I was filling the one or two penetrated laminae in the last of the pocks from machine-gun bullets as Erculo bolted the rear panel back in place. That was as much as we could do for now. The side window was a special-order item too. Anyway, it had fluxed fine.

The police van rolled into the lot. Lynx Feldshuh was driving. His face through the Spalltex windshield didn't have any expression at all.

The marshal kept his left hand in his pocket when he got out of his van. I didn't understand why until the twin turrets rotated and depressed. They were aimed square at the Lynx's back. If they fired, the storm of flame, machine-gun bullets, and missiles would sweep a path clear to the next county.

Hannah Martin wasn't along this time. The Lynx had rigged his weapons to a dead-man switch. If the marshal's left thumb released the switch—because my brother had shot him, for example—the police van's firepower would blow away the shop and everybody in it.

The Lynx walked straight to JC, who smiled at him. The clot of spectators looked from the marshal, to my brother— and finally to the van's turrets. *Then* the light dawned. I'd never seen fat old men move quicker.

Tires squealed in the parking lot. JC and the Lynx tried to look in two directions at once, watching each other but still seeing who the newcomer was.

It was Ditsy, driving her personal dune buggy instead of the TV truck. My brother and the marshal relaxed.

"Ditsy!" I shouted as I ran out of the workbay. She'd pulled up between the Lynx and his van. The dune buggy would vanish like a foil toy if the police flamethrower belched a rod of magnesium-enriched napalm.

"Don't worry, Brian," JC called to me. "Marshal Feldshuh and I are going to talk like reasonable gentlemen. Isn't that so, Lynx? You don't plan to fry your employer's daughter, do you?"

Ditsy was half out of the dune buggy with the minicam in her hand. She looked up at the broad, oval mouth of the flamethrower and raised an eyebrow. She walked over to where she could get both the Lynx and JC in her field of view, still well within the lethal range of the van's armaments.

I stood beside her, though there wasn't much call to, I suppose.

The Lynx grimaced. He took a flat case about the size of a cigarette pack from his left pocket and slid the integral clamp over the thumb-switch. Ditsy's presence had emptied the remote control's threat of total destruction.

In a way, you wouldn't think it would matter. If the van cut loose, the marshal himself was dead, after all. But JC was right about his man: Lynx Feldshuh wouldn't, as his final act, turn his employer's daughter into a crispy critter with a blast of napalm.

"All right, Deal," the Lynx said. "We'll talk. Let's talk about where you were last night."

"Let's talk about why you want to know," JC replied. He eyed the empty soda bottle in his hand, then lobbed it toward the trash barrel thirty feet away. The bottle disappeared into the barrel's maw with a ringing crash.

The marshal's lips tightened. He looked old and angry; not frightened, but frustrated like a bear that can't quite reach the dogs ringing it.

"Another Spike-K truck was knocked over this morning," he said at last. "Like the other one, a bike gang operating with a Q-car that made the actual kill."

The Lynx wiped his mouth with the back of his left hand. "Thing is, Deal," he went on, "the car that nailed the first truck handled just like your sedan . . . and like nothing else I know of in these parts."

"Well, I wish I could help you, Marshal," JC said, "but I didn't see any trucks where I was parked last night. I've been renewing old acquaintances in the area, you see. I don't think the lady would be real amused if I mentioned her name."

He grinned. "Nor would her husband, if he came to hear about it."

"Marshal," said Erculo unexpectedly from behind my shoulder, "let me show you the tractor we towed in yesterday."

He put his hand on Feldshuh's arm and led him firmly toward the wreck. I could tell that the Lynx didn't like the contact one bit—but he didn't like much about the current situation, and this at least provided a way to break clear of a confrontation with JC he'd obviously lost already.

Ditsy and I trailed the pair. Behind us, his thumbs hooked in his concho belt, came JC. After the scare from the dead-man switch, none of the idlers seemed willing to get close.

"Here," said Erculo, patting the gouge torn through the upper edge of the truck's bow armor. "The shot was aimed at the driver, but the weapon was mounted low—"

"On the centerline of a sedan, just like Deal's here is," the Lynx broke in.

"That is so," Erculo said. "The weapon was mounted low, so the shot hit first the four-inch armor here—"

The Lynx saw where the discussion was going. "It wasn't a square impact," he muttered. "It just nicked it."

JC reached past me and laid his clenched fist in the notch. The piece the shot blew out was big enough to hold my brother's big hand. "Right," he said. "Just a scratch."

Erculo climbed the mounting step and opened the cab door. "Come, Marshal," he said. "The shot then hit the armored windshield and shattered it completely. Then it went through the driver."

At so high a velocity that the fellow's chest *splashed* all over the interior of the cab, I thought.

"And then—do you see?" Erculo waggled his fingers in the hole in the rear wall of the cab.

We'd removed the driver's seat, and I'd hosed the vehicle off thoroughly this morning. Dozens of flies still rose when Erculo disturbed them.

"Out the back, which I admit isn't heavily armored, but still a two-inch hole," Erculo continued inexorably. "And into the semi-trailer itself. Yes?"

"I see that," said the Lynx, turning away. "But—"

"But Mr. Deal's sedan mounts a machine gun," Erculo said. "*Not* a cannon firing depleted-uranium shot weighing several pounds, which is what it would have taken to do this damage. With a velocity of two or three *miles* per second."

"You've got THE SQUARE DEAL on the rack still," JC suggested mildly. "I wouldn't mind the marshal here giving the old girl a once-over."

The Lynx looked at my brother without expression. "All right," the old man said. "Let's do that."

Ditsy hadn't said a word since her arrival. She was filming the whole discussion to use in later clips, perhaps with her own voice-over. JC touched a concho as we walked toward the bay. THE SQUARE DEAL's doors rose. Ditsy focused her minicam on the car.

The Lynx paused beside THE SQUARE DEAL. The mass of the flywheel, greasy-looking with the speed of its rotation, appeared to fascinate him.

"Go ahead, Marshal," JC offered. "The gun's in the console. Take off the access plate and get a good look."

The Lynx slid into the car. His movements were unexpectedly smooth and graceful, a sudden reminder of the old man's years in the arena. I watched from the other side as his fingers found the recessed dogs and twisted them to release the cover. Ditsy pushed against me to get the camera angle she wanted.

"As you see," JC added, "the flywheel doesn't leave much room for other hardware, though I've made do with what you see there. She's a fifteen-point-five-millimeter, built in Maine under license from FN in Belgium. Nice gun, isn't she?"

"But no doorknocker like it took to punch a hole through that rig," I put in, just to prove I was awake.

The Lynx used his index finger to guide his eyes over the workings of the big machine gun. He lifted the bolt a fraction of an inch against the hydraulic mechanism that would normally charge it for the first shot. The precisely-forged parts clacked like vault tumblers when he let the bolt slip back.

"Dual rate," JC said. "Six hundred and twelve hundred rpm. There's not much call for high rate out here"—he smiled—"'cept maybe the marshal's van."

It was an impressive gun. You could call it a light cannon if you wanted, instead of a heavy machine gun. But even with SLAP rounds, it couldn't have penetrated so much as the first layer of the truck's heavy armor with a single shot.

The Lynx got out of the car, looking at the bay's concrete floor in order to avoid meeting anyone's eyes. "That's what's here now, all right," he muttered.

Those were just words, not an argument. He was already looking for a path back to his car that wouldn't force him to face JC.

"Exactly, Marshal," my brother crowed. "One machine gun and a hundred rounds for it. *Only* a hundred, because that's all THE SQUARE DEAL's got room for without removing a seat—or the flywheel. Erculo, how long would it take you to fit my car with an anti-tank gun?''

Erculo shrugged. ''Ridiculous,'' he said. ''This car is built as a piece—hand-fitted, every part of it. Enlarge the tunnel, set back the flywheel. Cut the frontal armor or replace it with redesigned panels; the gunport is far too small.''

''I get the idea,'' the Lynx said. He strode past JC, careful not to touch him. Ditsy's camera whirred.

''The suspension would have to be changed to take the greater weight,'' Erculo continued, turning up a finger at each further point. ''And then the recoil besides.''

''Sorta like doing Mona Lisa as a blonde, Marshal,'' JC said to the Lynx's back. ''Getting the complexion right and the eyes too. Not just the hair.''

''I got my eye on you, Deal,'' the Lynx snapped as he climbed into the van. He pointedly *didn't* have his eye on JC, or me, or any of the idlers chuckling to see the rich man's law made to look a fool.

''About where I was, Marshal,'' JC called. ''It wasn't with Hannah, so you can rest easy on that score. Not last night, anyhow.''

The police van was too heavy to peel out of the parking area, but Lynx Feldshuh sure-god tried.

JC watched it leave with the expression a hawk gives a weasel: a meal if he wants it, but not without risk. Then my brother's face cleared into the mask of good humor it wore whenever he chose that it should. ''Erculo,'' he said, ''I'll give her a shakedown tonight, but I don't imagine there'll be any problems. I watched you work.''

Erculo beamed as he released the car, repaired in all but cosmetic details, from the clamps.

JC got in and closed the doors, then rolled down a window to look at me. "Brian," he said, "tell Ma not to wait supper for me. I've got business to attend."

All of us, Erculo and me and the dole-rats hoping for excitement in lives as bland as algae cake, watched THE SQUARE DEAL run northward up State 149.

CHAPTER 7

Mom held dinner that night until ten o'clock. She finally served it, but that meal was about as miserable a time as I'd spent in a long while. Mom cried all the way through.

Her John was back from the dead after twelve years and now she was losing him again. How could God be so cruel? If her John only understood the way he was breaking his mother's heart, he wouldn't go out like this at night.

JC had been eighteen when he left Mannheim. The age I was now.

Well, I wasn't JC. It didn't seem like I was anybody at all.

"I'm taking a walk, Mom," I said. I picked up my grenade launcher and checked to be sure the magazine was locked into its well.

The launcher Erculo had sold me—given me, really—

came from a wreck whose owners didn't need hardware anymore. It was Singapore-made and three-shot, designed for smaller people who didn't want the weight of five 40mm grenades in a loaded magazine.

Well, I'm not very big myself. Besides, because the weapon was clip- rather than tube-fed—a five-round box magazine for grenades was unusably awkward—the balance didn't change when I fired.

"You're going to see that girl again, aren't you?" Mom said. She was still bent over her plate; her food was untouched. I'd have offered to do the dishes before I left, but I knew she wouldn't let me.

"I don't know, Mom," I said. I slung the bandolier of reloads over my left shoulder. No particular reason. "I may go to the studio. Ditsy may be there."

Ditsy *may* be willing to see me . . . but I didn't say that out loud. I wasn't sure how Ditsy felt about the Deal family just now.

To my surprise, Mom didn't object. She went back to sniffling over JC's absence.

I was going to bang the screen door as I left. I changed my mind and caught it just before it hit, easing it down against the pull of the spring.

Mannheim was quiet at night. Heck, Mannheim is quiet most times. We get a few truckers overnighting, but they need to be on the road the next morning. Sometimes a crew from the Spike-K comes in to party, but even that has tended to be pretty sedate since the Lynx and his van came on the scene.

The bandolier chafed my left shoulder. Times were that I might've been hassled by Terry and the Pirates when I walked to the highway in the center of town, then north to the TV station. Not anymore. . . .

There were two cars parked by K660 when I got there. One was the compact owned by Red Elwanger, the regular night engineer; the other was Ditsy's dune buggy. The TV truck was garaged beside the building, locked up tight to prevent kids from borrowing the heavy vehicle to bulldoze the center of town.

Ditsy didn't have a job, exactly. Better, she had any job at the station she wanted, and none of the people Big Ben hired to manage K660 were going to tell her different. Her father would have been just as happy if Ditsy had called herself Dorothea, the name she'd been baptized, and decided to be a lady who raised the tone of Mannheim.

But that wasn't her, and she was too much Big Ben's daughter for him to stand in the way if she really wanted to work.

Besides, Ditsy *was* a darned good reporter. Big Ben liked his operations to run well.

I reached for the doorbell, wondering how long I'd wait if the door didn't open. There was a closed-circuit camera above the door for security. Ditsy hadn't spoken to me at the shop that morning, and I wasn't sure she was going to feel different about it later.

The door opened before I touched the bell. "Hello, Brian," Ditsy said. "I was getting worried that you weren't going to come."

I cleared my throat. "Ah . . . ," I said. "Ah, dinner was late."

"Come look at a clip of the hijacking this morning," Ditsy said, trotting back into the studio on the assumption that I'd lock the door and follow her . . . like I always did. She must have been watching the security camera to get to the door for me that way.

I nodded at Red in the control room. He was an old man; bald with a toothbrush mustache, and that was white. Red was a top engineer when he was sober, and good enough drunk to get by. I don't recall seeing him more than twice that he didn't at least have a buzz on. I guess the booze was a shame, but that and Red's total lack of ambition were all that kept him working in a one-horse town like Mannheim.

He grinned and gave me the high sign. I guess Red thought more was going on between me and Ditsy than really was. Maybe it was just wishful thinking on his part.

"It's from a hundred thirty miles west of here on the Interstate," Ditsy was explaining as she cued up the recording on a monitor. "We wouldn't normally get the feed, but I bought the rights special."

"Expensive?" I asked, mostly to be saying something.

"No, of course not," Ditsy snapped, like I'd asked if the sun was up yet. "Minimum payment. There's no entertainment value in it at all."

The recording started to run, dim pictures from the cab and tail turret of what I assumed was a tractor/semi combination because of the wide difference in the cameras' oscillation patterns. Another rig was six or seven hundred yards ahead of the one feeding us.

"They're eastbound, coming toward us," Ditsy commented. She liked to know the details, even when they didn't seem to matter. It was hard to know what *did* matter in this business.

In the left lane, a quarter mile back of the tail turret, was a gray sedan. I could just about make out dim glimpses of bikes in the far distance behind the car.

"According to the driver of the lead rig," Ditsy said, "the sedan called on his CB to say that he was being followed by a bike gang and could he please tuck in between the rigs for safety.''

"Truckers aren't in the business of taking care of civilians," I muttered.

"That's what they thought, too," Ditsy said. "The rig drivers switched channels and made plans of their own."

The rig that was feeding us began to close up with the leading vehicle. The sedan held station but didn't attempt to pass without permission. The dumbest civilian knew *that* was suicide.

"The truckers decided to line up abreast," Ditsy went on. "That way they'd both have their full tail armament to bear."

"They're hoping the bikers will settle for the sedan and leave their rigs alone," I said. "Sorta like throwing the baby out the back of the sleigh to the wolf pack."

"That's what they thought they were doing, all right," Ditsy agreed mildly. "Keep watching."

I could understand what the truckers were doing, but I didn't much like it. The data crawl put a 7.62mm Gatling and a 30mm automatic cannon in the tail blister of the rig feeding us. I could see a rocket pod on the trailer ahead. All that, plus heavy dropped-weapons packages, was enough to handle a bike gang twenty times over.

But truckers weren't paid to take chances, and they weren't paid to protect civilians. If the poor sucker in the sedan thought he needed a rig to protect him from bike dirt, then he should have been driving a rig. . . .

I remembered Marshal Feldshuh saying the hijacked rig wore the Spike-K emblem. "Did Kames own both of the rigs?" I asked.

Ditsy shook her head. "The other rig's a gypsy. The

driver was alone, trying to cut costs by not carrying a gunner.''

The images on the split screen shifted as the Spike-K driver angled his tractor into the left lane. The articulated load followed fractionally slower, so for a moment the truck's cab was in the left lane while most of the semi was still in the right.

The sedan following the rigs bucked in the cloud of glowing plasma expelled from its centerline weapon. The left side of the monitor blanked as the projectile severed the camera's leads as it blasted through the massively-armored cab of the tractor.

Tracers danced crazily across the right-side image as the rig's tail gunner thumbed his triggers. The Gatling ripped out a red-orange ribbon while the autocannon spewed huge glowing pearls at the rate of one to twenty of the Gatling's 6,000 machine-gun rounds per minute.

The gunner raked the air, the road, and the empty landscape to either side. The rig was fishtailing wildly as it plowed across the median. If any of the shells and bullets hit their intended target, it was pure chance and the sedan's armor shrugged them off.

The last recorded image was a view of tracers streaming skyward. The machine gun bullets burned out at about a thousand yards, but 30mm shells sailed up almost into the clouds before they vanished.

There was no doubt that the impact that smashed the camera had also killed the gunner.

''Just like the one the other day,'' I said.

''One shot, one rig,'' Ditsy agreed. ''No entertainment value at all.''

I backed the recording and froze the image on the sedan

just before it fired. There wasn't anything more to see; just the snout of a scared civilian's car, as gray as the night and blurred further by the optics of the cheap camera doing the recording.

"It's not a duel, it's not a fight," Ditsy said. "It's just murder. And it's been going on for years."

I looked at her in surprise. *"This?"* I said, unfreezing the image. The plasma discharge lit the night like a thunderbolt. "No, we'd have heard about it."

"That," Ditsy said. She waved a sheaf of hard copy at me.

"And we don't hear about it," she went on. "It doesn't make the vids because there's nothing interesting about it—except that it happens. So does sunrise, and nobody tries to sell TV advertising with films of *that*. I've got the records here of over a hundred hijacks over the past ten years. Every six months or so, the gang switches its base of operations, but it's still one gang."

I took the off-prints from her hand. Even a quick glance proved that Ditsy was right. Rig after rig, sniped and stripped.

I riffled through the hard-copy. Ditsy had done a computer sort for rigs whose cabs were burned after a hijacking. To hide evidence of one-shot kills—and as long as the thermite grenades went off, it *did* hide the evidence. You couldn't tell much from a fuzzy video if you hadn't seen the incredible result. All the incidents in that category were as similar as pearls on a wire—which wasn't really surprising, since I wouldn't have believed there were any such attacks until I'd watched the hit two nights before on the Interstate.

The attacks started in upstate New York, then zigzagged across the South and Midwest. There were no more than ten hijacks in any particular region. The attacks would stop for a time; then, after a few months of silence, there'd be another spate in a node centered hundreds of miles away from the previous batch.

"This is sick," I muttered.

Ditsy nodded agreement. "It's like reading about a hundred icepick murders," she said. "None of them had a chance."

Her face slipped into the hard, professional mask that I'd seen more and more of as Ditsy grew older. "And," she went on, "it's a story. A *big* story."

I shrugged. "It's a big business, at least," I said.

"Umm?"

I ran my finger down the column of the printout where the losses were tabulated. "This isn't a bike gang snatching what it can and maybe trading the surplus with other outlaws," I explained. "All of these trailers were stripped, whether they were loaded with cabbages or washing machines. That takes trucks and organization—and it means the gang's operating in the cash economy, not living in a cave."

Ditsy understood. "The way they're disposing of the loot," she said, "has to be as professional as the hijackings themselves are."

I remembered the damage to the rig in Erculo's yard. Dense armor spiked through like tissue, as if a meteor had struck the cab. A velocity of two or three *miles* per second, Erculo had said.

"Sure," I muttered to myself. "Nobody built a weapon like *that* in their garage."

Ditsy opened her mouth, probably to ask what I meant. The alarm rang.

I didn't know what the chime meant. Red Elwanger sat up straight in the control room. Ditsy immediately plugged her headset into the console and began typing commands. The monitor screen switched from the recording of the hijack to a street map of Mannheim. A yellow highlight pulsed over the Security Warehouse icon.

"Come on, Red!" Ditsy shouted as she stripped off her headset. "There's a break-in at Dad's warehouse! You drive and I'll man the camera!"

She ran to the equipment locker by the door and threw it open. There were four suits of ceramic back-and-breast armor inside, plus pistols and automatic rifles. Ditsy grabbed the smallest set of armor and one of the pistols. "Come *on*, Red!" she repeated. "Get your armor and let's go!"

Red opened the door of the control room. "Sorry, missy," he said. "Not me. I'm a studio engineer, not a gunman."

"Your job is—" Ditsy blazed.

"My job isn't worth my life, missy," Red said. "Sorry."

Ditsy hadn't belted on her pistol yet. I thought she might throw it at the old man.

"Ditsy," I said. "I'll go. But I want you to drive."

Ditsy's hair whipped as she turned to me. "You!" she blazed. "What do you know about framing shots, Brian? You drive."

It used to be I was afraid of Ditsy when she blazed out with orders and scorn for anybody too slow in obeying. "No, Ditsy," I said. "You drive with me in the bucket, or you drive alone. It's your choice."

I didn't say I wanted her behind the truck's armor instead of up in the cherrypicker, but I guess she knew.

She blinked. "Draw some armor, Brian," she said as she headed for the door to the garage. "We're late already."

Behind us, Red took a long drink from a pint flask.

CHAPTER 8

We highballed through Mannheim to the alarm site. The cherrypicker was locked in its cradle, but it still swayed more than I'd expected up on top of the truck. I bounced around the bucket like a pea in a whistle as I latched the clamshell armor around me.

I put on the communications helmet lying on the floor of the bucket. It was connected by a length of flex to the camera mount. A lighted keypad there gave a choice of CB channels, and a lever on the helmet itself switched between CB and intercom. I chose the former and set the panel on SEARCH.

There were two explosions from south of town, toward the warehouse. The first was short and as sharp as a rifle shot, only a thousand times louder. I figured it for the shaped-charge warhead of an anti-tank rocket.

The second bang was duller but still plenty loud. The

low clouds lit with an unpleasant yellowish-pink that I recognized as the signature of Fibrex. Nothing unusual about
that. Fibrex was both more stable and more powerful than
the dynamite folks used in the past generation. I don't guess
there was a farm around Mannheim that didn't have some
Fibrex on hand for anything from stumping to channeling
adobe soil for a new water line.

That didn't mean Fibrex couldn't be used for a weapon,
though.

In the pitching darkness, I eased back my launcher's bolt
to check the dimples on the case head of the round in the
chamber. The stamped pattern indicated the type of grenade.
This one was what it ought to be, three dots: dual purpose,
shaped-charge armor-piercing with fragmentation effect.

You couldn't be too careful.

Big Ben Wallace's Grenadier limousine made a screeching turn from Liberty Street and led us south down the highway. The police van fell in behind at the intersection, putting
the TV truck in the middle of an impromptu convoy. I won't
say I was sorry for the company when I saw what was waiting
for us at the warehouse.

A lighted chain-link fence surrounded Security Warehouse. Big Ben kept two men on duty at all times, both as
guards and to accept freight at odd hours. Security Warehouse
provided a lockup corral for rigs. A fair amount of the warehouse's business came from truckers who decided to catch
some rack time but wanted better security for their cargo than
they could get in the parking lot of the usual nap trap.

The lights were still on, all but the one on the pole
knocked down when a half-tracked five-ton drove through the
fence. The half-track ordinarily carried supplies to outlying
camps during Spike-K roundups. That was pretty much what

was going on here too, because Stannard Kames and his whole crew were here at the warehouse.

The half-track was strictly a work vehicle and unarmed. (Well, the cab roof carried a machine gun on a Scarff ring, but that's pretty much like saying the half-track had windshield wipers. Some things you take for granted.) There was no lack of armament on the dozen Spike-K pickups, though, facing out from the warehouse doors like a herd of angry buffalo. They had full crews and their motors were running.

The heavy doors of the warehouse hung open but askew. Cowboys were ransacking the brilliantly lighted interior. I remembered the pair of explosions and understood how the Spike-K crew had forced entry.

After the half-track had bulled through the fence, Kames' CHIEF had fired one of its pair of wire-guided missiles into the door where the leaves met. A blast powerful enough to blow in the warehouse doors would have flattened most of the houses in Mannheim, but the shaped-charge warhead of the anti-tank missile burned a hole through the panel.

One of Kames' men then packed in as much Fibrex as the hole would take and detonated it. The internal explosion crumpled the doors and flung them open. The trick was nothing new to the cowboys. They'd probably used the same technique a hundred times before to make roadcuts and shatter rock for gravel on the ranch.

There hadn't been any shots during the break-in. I understood why when I saw that the whole Spike-K crew was present, at least thirty men. The warehousemen hadn't figured Big Ben paid them enough to commit suicide for him.

The pickups were backed against the fenceline in a tight arc. Their guns and bow armor faced outward. Cowboy guns tracked our three heavy vehicles as we arrived, but they didn't open fire the way I thought they might.

I hunched down in the cherrypicker, hoping nobody noticed me. The bucket would stop machine-gun bullets, at least the first few of them, but it was just as dangerous a spot as I'd figured when I refused to let Ditsy take it.

Ditsy would spit like a wet cat when she learned I hadn't been filming. I guessed I could take that so long as I was alive to listen.

"Feldshuh!" Big Ben snarled over the radio. "I thought you were supposed to be the law around here! Where in blazes have you been?"

Kames' boys were monitoring the CB, so there wasn't any way for Wallace and the Lynx to have a private conversation. It didn't sound like Big Ben *wanted* a private conversation. He seemed more in a mood to spit than speak.

"I'm here now, Mr. Wallace," the marshal's transmission crackled from the blue-and-white van. "I swung by to pick up my deputy. This isn't a business to go into half-crewed."

I noticed that Big Ben *didn't* start shooting, nor order the Lynx to open the dance either.

A man ran out of the building. He was one of the green-uniformed warehousemen. The cowboys had left the fellow his body armor, though his pistol holster flopped empty on his hip. He paused at the outward-facing arm of Spike-K vehicles, but one of Kames' men waved him on curtly.

The warehouseman ran to Wallace's car. The off-side window, out of the potential line of fire, hissed down. I rose in the bucket to hear them better.

"They just bust in, Mr. Wallace!" the warehouseman gabbled. "There wasn't nothing me nor Willie could do. They

said they was looking for their prope'ty, but when they found
it there was gonna be the Devil to pay!''

Big Ben made an instant decision that said a lot for his
courage, though maybe not so much for his common sense.
The big car's rear door opened and a ramp lowered. Big Ben
whined down it, onto the apron of the warehouse. The muzzle
of CHIEF's 30mm cannon wasn't but ten yards from his chest.

''Kames!'' Wallace roared. ''What d'ye think you're
playing at? There's none of your goods in this warehouse. It'd
stink up the rest of my stock too bad!''

Stannard Kames got out of his pickup. He'd been driving
CHIEF himself, though there was a ranch hand beside him in
the cab. The rancher's broad-brimmed hat shadowed him
faceless in the lights mounted on high standards, but there
was no mistaking his spare figure or his voice.

''I say we will find my property here, Wallace!'' Kames
shouted. ''I don't reckon it was an accident that both rigs got
knocked over were mine, and I don't reckon their cargo just
vanished into thin air, neither. So I asked myse'f, if I was a
crooked warehouse-owning SOB who hated Stannard Kames,
what would I do with the loot I stole from him?''

A vehicle pulled away from the Spike-K lineup. I jumped
out of a year's growth, but it was only the supply half-track.
The missile rack on the rear of the police van followed the
vehicle for only a moment before swinging back to cover the
pickup mounting twin 20mm Gatlings.

The half-track squealed and clattered off into the darkness across the highway. It looked to me like somebody'd
decided to take himself and the unarmed, barely armored vehicle out of the line of fire. That made such good sense that
not even Stannard Kames seemed to mind.

When the sound of the half-track faded, Big Ben Wallace

said in a deadly voice, ''You'll find no contraband in my warehouse, Kames. And I want you to know that the time is past when a rancher's armed thugs could terrorize a community. There's a posse coming down from Welborn and Cross Creek. You're going to pay for the damage you've done here tonight.''

A cowboy ran out the warehouse doorway. ''Chief!'' he bawled. ''Chief! We found it! Three cases of ammo with lot numbers from the manifest of the first truck they hijacked! We found the loot!''

You could feel trigger fingers tightening in the darkness.

CHAPTER 9

The gun-shield of an automatic grenade launcher screeched. The weapon was mounted in the second stake-hole on the pickup's side, so close to the cab that armor rubbed armor when the cowboy sighted on Big Ben.

"No!" said Stannard Kames like the crack of a whip-lash. The rancher's knobbed, powerful hand made a chopping motion to the men behind him.

"Mr. Wallace," ordered the Lynx. His voice was controlled but hoarse with tension. "Get in your car fast. Head *south*."

Both Big Ben's car and the police van—as well as our truck—were pointed south. Running in that direction would save turning around and put the Lynx between his boss and the pursuit.

The downside was that the nearest town in that direction was Yellow Water, if you call that a town, a hundred and twenty miles away. Maintenance on State 149 went to loads of gravel between potholes, and the scrub to either side of the road was Spike-K grazing land.

The marshal was a pro. He'd looked at a bad situation and come up with the best plan he could. I didn't figure Big Ben Wallace would go along with it, though. The Lynx was willing to bet that he could keep the cowboys off his boss's back during a long run to nowhere, but Wallace would be thinking of his fortified home. . . .

Big Ben backed his wheelchair without turning. His left wheel squeaked against the ramp's low coaming. Wallace paused and eased forward again, then straightened the chair without going over.

Nobody else moved. Stannard Kames stood like a haughty statue.

The six-wheeled pickup with a pair of rocket pods on its shelltop was too well armored to be a good target for my grenade launcher, but those fourteen-pound warheads were the heaviest ordnance aimed at the TV truck.

Better a bad chance than no chance at all. I eased my weapon over the edge of the bucket, pointed it at the sighting head between the rocket pods, and squeezed the targeting switch with my thumb.

A tiny infrared laser, invisible to me as well as everybody else, pinged the target. Some of the coherent light bounced back to the receiving lens beside the emitter in the launcher's fore-end, giving a precise range. My rear sights sank automatically. I steadied the weapon, bringing the three-dot pattern, front spur between rear forks, into precise alignment.

Of course, I should've been able to hit the target blind-folded, with it only forty feet away.

The wheelchair's drive motor flung Big Ben backwards into his limousine. The car wheels began to spray gravel in a tight turn even before the Grenadier's door slammed like a bank vault. Big Ben was heading home, just like I figured.

The police van swung out simultaneously—and blocked the limo, maybe by accident. Big Ben's chauffeur hauled the wheel to the right in a jagged S and headed south again.

Stannard Kames waited until Wallace's limousine was accelerating out of its turn. The rancher slid under the steering wheel of his pickup. I noticed out of the corner of my eye how Kames kept the thickness of the truck's armored door between him and the police van's front turret until he could close it behind him.

Not that the door would have been much help if shooting started. Deputy Martin's hose of napalm would splash and flow, sucking air from the rancher's lungs as it melted his flesh.

But the shooting didn't start. The cowboys who'd been turning over Security Warehouse ran out of the building in nervous pairs and trios, jumping aboard their pickups. None of the Spike-K vehicles moved.

The warehouseman who'd talked to Big Ben looked naked in the glaring headlights of the TV truck. He suddenly ran across the road to disappear into the anonymous darkness.

Ditsy cramped the truck's steering wheel. She'd nosed into the warehouse driveway and had to back and fill to get onto the highway. If a front wheel slid into the ditch, it was long odds the heavy truck would stick there. There was better than a fair chance that we'd roll over, grinding me into the soil unless I managed to jump from the cherrypicker in time.

The police van's all-wheel steering let it maneuver easily to follow the limo. The two turrets swiveled in unison to keep the flamethrower and missile pod aligned with the Spike-K crew.

Kames *still* didn't act. The police van accelerated down State 149 while Ditsy whimpered curses over the intercom as she slammed our truck into reverse, then forward again with the cherrypicker wobbling dangerously.

I saw it out of the corner of my eye: a gray, straight-sided shadow lying across the road in the police van's headlights. The Spike-K half-track hadn't run away after all. Its crew had unrolled a mat of Fibrex, six feet wide and I couldn't guess how long, as they crossed the dark highway in the direction our vehicles were headed. They must have used the ranch's whole stock of the explosive.

The limousine's tires had mussed the edges of the mat. Kames let Big Ben cross the improvised minefield because he knew he could finish Wallace any time—once the Lynx was out of the way.

The marshal saw the Fibrex when I did—but no sooner. He was driving with one eye and keeping the other on the Spike-K vehicles motionless in the targeting display of the van's rear turret.

I hadn't appreciated just how good the Lynx was until that moment. Instead of hitting the brakes and skidding over the mat before his heavy vehicle could halt, he kept the accelerator rammed to the firewall. The police van was halfway clear of the Fibrex before Stannard Kames detonated it.

I figure Kames meant the explosion to be the signal for the shooting war to start. I beat him by the time it took to squeeze my trigger and duck down in my bucket.

The flash of yellow-pink light was as bright as sunrise. Kames' men were cowboys, not duelists, and they were using the commercial explosive they had on hand instead of anti-armor mines for which the ranch had no need. Not surprisingly, they underestimated both the resistance of the police van to an omnidirectional blast—and the effect that blast would have on lighter vehicles, like their own.

All *I* knew was that the pressure pulse dished in the front of the bucket, squashed the air from my lungs, and lifted the cherrypicker arm to 45° before the hydraulic struts twisted immobile. The only thing that saved me and the cherrypicker from being torn off and hurled hundreds of feet was the bluff slope of the truck cab. The blast was at ground level, so the cab's heavy armor diverted the worst of the shockwave over me.

The hundreds of pounds of Fibrex blew grit out from the explosion's center in a rectangular doughnut. It hurled gunshields and cowboys from the open beds of pickups like a line-straight battering ram, into the chain-link fence an instant before the supporting poles broke or ripped out of the ground. Men, equipment, and the steel meshes flailed through the air together until the whole mass smashed into the front of the warehouse.

On the south end of the Spike-K semicircle, closest to the explosion, was a light four-by-four. It flipped end for end. The other pickups withstood the blast by rocking back on their suspensions, but their shockwave-stunned crews didn't react with the instant volley Kames intended.

I meant my grenade to hit the periscopic sight between the paired seven-rocket pods on the Spike-K pickup. In anticipation of the Fibrex going off, I twitched and pulled my shot to the left. Instead of the sight, my grenade blew up on the nose of one of the Spike-K rockets.

The rocket's warhead detonated, setting off the whole array—fourteen-pound warheads and the solid rocket fuel besides—in a dazzling secondary explosion. An orange fireball so intense you could have walked on it expanded in all directions.

The shelltop flattened to the truck bed. The six-wheeler's springs compressed, then flung the vehicle up into the vacuum blasted from the air by the explosion. The pickup landed on its side, bounced, and rolled upside down. No one tried to get out of the wreckage.

The police van's undercarriage was wedge-shaped and thickly armored to limit mine damage. "Limit" couldn't mean "prevent" when the vehicle was on top of so much Fibrex. The rear of the seven-ton van lifted like the legs of a child attempting to somersault. All four of the back wheels flew off.

When the rear end crashed down again, the van continued to skid forward on inertia. Magenta sparks spewed to either side as the undercarriage rubbed against gravel mixed into the highway's asphaltic concrete. The marshal fought for control, unaware of the extent of his vehicle's damage.

I raised up in the bucket. I had a better view than before because the cherrypicker was jammed higher. Everything was motion and the harsh muzzle flashes of guns firing through the haze.

I would have heard screaming if the explosions hadn't numbed my ears.

The Spike-K's heavy six-by-sixes, three of them since my hit on the rocket warhead had eliminated the fourth, were built to take the punishment dished out by the Fibrex and the secondary explosion of their fellow. The 120mm recoilless rifle of one belched a huge, bottle-shaped flare from the muzzle and an even greater fan of backblast out the vent in the rear of the shelltop's turret. The vent had a slight upward angle, but it still singed the eyebrows of cowboys in the beds of open pickups nearby.

The big shell went off a thousand yards down the highway, close enough to its target that the red flash lighted Big Ben's limousine like a flare. The car fishtailed wildly, from damage or just the concussion.

Meanwhile, another six-by-six accelerated onto the highway while its paired 20mm Gatlings raked the police van from back to broadside.

The guns drew fluctuating ribbons of yellow fire, smashing and sparkling across the target. The night throbbed with their deep bass note. The six laser-guided missiles in the van's rear turret disintegrated in the storm of armor-piercing shot. Fragments of casing, warhead, and fuel from the solid rocket motors—some of it burning—flew out like chips from a circle saw.

Despite the awesome weight of fire, the oblique angle and massive armor saved the van long enough for Hannah Martin to lurch upright in her restraints and trigger the flamethrower. The rod of napalm, red and diamond-white with sparks of magnesium, caught the Spike-K vehicle at the end of a flat, forty-yard arc.

The pickup had fireproof armor. The shelltop didn't. The flame rod struck the truck's windshield to spray up and outward. The shelltop's turret sagged like a wave-swept sand castle. The tailgate flew open. The gunner threw himself out, ablaze even before he was clear of the doomed vehicle.

20mm ammunition began to burn inside the truck bed, a rattling hammer still quicker than the Gatlings' own 12,000-rounds-per-minute rate. Tracers whizzed out the open tailgate like sparks from a Roman candle. The remainder of the load detonated, bulging the sides of the pickup and flinging it across the road in front of our truck. Ditsy skidded to a halt.

Most of the Spike-K pickups sped out of the semicircle like a covey of quail rising, chasing after Big Ben Wallace as fast as their blast-shocked drivers could respond. CHIEF, with Stannard Kames in its driver's seat, remained motionless.

CHIEF's turret traversed to follow the limousine, but the long 30mm cannon didn't fire. Kames' gunner had launched one of his two missiles to hole the warehouse door. Downrange, wobbling like a huge saffron firefly, I saw the flare pot of the second missile homing in on Wallace's car as the gunner fed signals to the flight controls down a hair-thin optical fiber "wire."

I fired at CHIEF's turret, snap shooting because the target was close and there wasn't any time to aim. So far as I was concerned, anything but the limo and the police van was a target. Ditsy threw the truck into gear again just as I squeezed off. My grenade burst with a *flash*/crack! on the pavement beyond the six-by-six, too far away for the patter of its piano-wire shrapnel to startle the gunner off his mark—which was as much as I'd hoped to do, given CHIEF's heavy armor.

It was too late for that anyway. Even as I squeezed off, the tracking flare intersected the speeding limousine. The warhead of the wire-guided missile lit neighboring fields yellow. The hollow *tock* of the explosion echoed over us four seconds later.

Wallace's car spun twice in a pall of dust. When the limousine reappeared on the far side of the dust cloud, it was crawling along like a crippled insect. The anti-tank missile had blown off the left rear wheel. It was a tribute to Grenadier, the manufacturer, that the limousine could still move on three wheels—

But it didn't move very well, or very fast. Though the car disappeared around a curve in the highway, it wouldn't take too long for Kames' men to catch up again with Big Ben.

The ranch hands had expected their Fibrex minefield to destroy the police van. When it didn't—and the twin Gatlings didn't do the job either—the turret gunners in the surviving six-by-sixes knew they *personally* had a problem, because the Lynx and his deputy were certain to direct their fire at the most dangerous opponents.

CHIEF's turret and the 120mm in the other vehicle had been following the limousine. Now both pickups swung their weapons toward the hopelessly crippled van as they drove past. Reloading the big recoilless was a job slower than molasses in January—each round of ammunition was heavy and four feet long. CHIEF's 30mm cannon spat bright green tracers into the police vehicle's broadside.

The van's rear turret was canted up in the first stage of being reloaded with missiles to replace those the Gatlings had destroyed before Marshal Feldshuh could use them. Hannah's front-turret flamethrower slammed a hose of fire into CHIEF while her co-ax machine gun twinkled.

Kames' pickup rocked from the impact of ten gallons of metal-enriched napalm. Red and sparkling white flames boomed up and back in CHIEF's slipstream, covering both the windshield and the cannon sights.

Unlike the Gatling-equipped shelltop, Kames' personal vehicle was entirely fireproof. The rod of blazing napalm still blinded him and his gunner. CHIEF staggered and lost its line though the rancher continued to accelerate. 30mm shells spat out in a high arc over the scrubland.

The other six-by-six, leading CHIEF by a hundred yards, rocked up onto the highway. The 120mm recoilless was trained over the left rear quarter, straight at the police van's windshield. I figured the big squash-head projectile would blow that windshield and frontal plate about midway through the vehicle's body. Hannah Martin traversed the front turret toward it—but not fast enough, and the 200 yards between van and pickup was probably outside the flamethrower's range.

The Lynx fired the eight-inch bombardment rocket in the police van's left-side launching trough.

When the twin Gatlings had gnawed the van like a school of piranhas, the sleeting projectiles had shredded the right-side launcher and the multiple flechette rockets podded there. The hundred-pound warhead of the bombardment rocket, protected on the far side of the van, was better for a massive target like the six-by-six anyway.

The weapon was unguided, but the Lynx hadn't lost his touch for timing with a low-deflection target. Backblast from the launcher blew a vast ring of dust in the direction of Mannheim while the rocket sprang smoothly from its trough. The rocket was still accelerating when it hit the pickup.

The Spike-K vehicle vanished behind a red fireball. A fraction of a second later, ten or a dozen rounds for the 120mm gun went off in a secondary explosion that sent panels of thick body armor flapping through the night like batwings. A column of smoke and dust twisted hundreds of feet into the sky. It topped out in an anvil shape that rained bits of the pickup.

Bits of the pickup—and its crew. A human torso slapped down onto the roadway to lie in the fan of our headlights. Ditsy drove over it.

I switched to intercom. "Ditsy!" I screamed. "This isn't a tank, it's a camera truck!"

There were at least half a dozen Spike-K pickups in the

direction we were headed. Any one of them could chew us to bits, given time and the inclination. The TV truck carried only single fore-and-aft machine guns for armament, so the ranch hands had been too busy with dangerous targets to worry about it.

As soon as they realized that the big vehicle bore the K660 logo, they'd be inclined to find the time. . . .

"He's my father!" Ditsy screamed back. "Get off if you haven't the balls!"

Jumping from as high as the bucket was raised would have been about as dangerous as anything Ditsy was going to drive us into. It wasn't me I was worried about, anyway. It was her . . . but the decision was out of my hands.

CHAPTER 10

We wallowed across the crater the six-by-six had torn in the road when it disintegrated. State 149 south of Mannheim wasn't exactly a turnpike on its best day. The cherrypicker whipped back and forth. I'd been worried that the arm might break. Now I started to wonder if the oscillation was going to fling me out.

The Spike-K vehicles spread into a broad skirmish line to either side of the road. It was pretty obvious that the limousine wasn't going to be running far, but it still had teeth. After his trouble with the laser guidance system of his previous car, Big Ben had mounted a pod of hypervelocity rockets on its replacement. They could turn any of the pickups—except maybe CHIEF, *maybe*—into Swiss cheese. Bunching up in a big target would be suicide.

Besides, the cowboys needed to cover a wide area. There was a good chance Big Ben was going to get out and try to go cross-country in his wheelchair while his chauffeur drew fire in the limousine. Stannard Kames was reckoning to settle the score between them once and for all.

The ranch vehicles bounced through the scrub at as good a rate as Ditsy made along the road. The four-by-fours were built for the job, and their drivers probably had more experience off-road than they did of highway driving.

Because we were big and were moving, pickups opened fire on us. Mostly it was machine-gun fire. The bullets ricocheted harmlessly from the truck's thick armor, though any one of the wild shots snapping through the air would be enough to fix *my* wagon.

The gunfire would have been a lot heavier and more dangerous except for the damage the Fibrex had done to the Spike-K vehicles. The tremendous shockwave had put paid to at least half the weapon stations and crews on the back of open pickups.

A truck 200 yards to the left raked us with a ten-round burst from its automatic grenade launcher. Most of the grenades flashed beside and behind us, but two went off against the side of the truck with hollow *klocks*. Bits of piano wire zeeped harmlessly through the air.

The shaped-charge warheads might or might not penetrate our side armor. Since there was nobody in the body of the vehicle, the tiny jets of superheated gas weren't going to do any harm unless a grenade hit the cab.

I fired back with the last round in my magazine and reloaded. This time I shoved in a clip of white phosphorus grenades. They were meant as marking rounds. Each threw out a huge blob of white smoke when it went off, so that other gunners could concentrate their fire on the indicated target.

JC had shown me Willie Pete had other uses.

The belt-fed automatic in the pickup opened up again. The gunner had raised his point of aim, but he still wasn't leading us by enough. Four of the grenades hit us, but they all burst on the rear half of the truck.

My bucket was an even worse weapons platform than the bed of a pickup pitching through scrub, but I'd spent as much time shooting reloadable practice grenades as I had on Er- culo's driving simulator. I aimed by instinct, leading by sev- eral vehicle lengths to compensate for the grenades' low velocity, about 250 feet per second.

I fired on the cherrypicker's upswing and fired again while the first round was still in the air. A pair of machine- gun bullets whacked the side of my bucket. One screamed off into the night. The other penetrated and danced around the interior in a spray of red sparks. It kicked my right foot side- ways, and I twitched the last round in the magazine skyward.

My first grenade sailed just over the four-by-four's cab and raised a Christmas tree of white smoke in the scrub. Sere grass began to burn sullenly. The second round landed where I wanted it, squarely in the pickup's open bed.

A dual-purpose grenade like those I'd been firing before might have killed a gunner if I'd gotten a lucky hit square on him. The ranch hands who'd survived the Fibrex explosion were all in good body armor, though. Miniature shrapnel blown from the grenade's wire-wound case wouldn't cause serious casualties.

Bits of blazing phosphorus couldn't be ignored the way prickles of wire in the unprotected lower legs would be.

There were three men in the back of the pickup, two of them firing at us with a machine gun and the automatic gre- nade launcher, while the third was ready to take over a gun if anything happened to its present crew. A tiny bursting

charge ruptured the casing and threw out phosphorus parti-
cles, each spewing its own smoke trail. For an instant the
gray-white smoke enfolded the cowboys in tentacles like an
octopus.

Whirling like dervishes, the ranch hands flung themselves out of the back of the truck together, as though they'd
rehearsed the timing. For a few moments, the dense cloud
clung to the box as the four-by-four bounced on. Pale flames
lighted the heart of it as the phosphorus found flammables it
could ignite.

Machine gun ammo began to cook off with a popping
rattle. Tracers whizzed around the truck box like minuscule
lighted buzzsaws. Bullets propelled by ruptured cases instead
of chambers and gun-barrels were no threat even to the light
armor of a working four-by-four, but the ripping commotion
must have been terrifying to the crew in the cab.

Then the box of 40mm grenades went off. The bed of
the pickup flew apart in a red flash. The cab flipped end for
end several times and came to rest upside down. One of the
doors opened. A cowboy flopped out, but he didn't move
from where he lay.

The pickup on the eastern end of the Spike-K skirmish
line trailed back from the others because of the time it had
taken the driver to reach his outlying position. That position
gave the crew a good view of what had happened to their
fellow, so they decided to even the score. The machine gunner in the cab wasn't a serious threat at 600 yards—

But the post-mounted 30mm cannon in the truck box was
something else again.

The first shell was a flaming onion that sailed over us.
The second hit our truck just behind the cab and burst like
the crack of doom. The third, thank God, was short—but not

very short, and the heavier shrapnel from its casing struck quick hammer blows to our armor.

The gun was a medium-velocity weapon, not a long-barreled can-opener like the one in CHIEF's turret. Even so, the thirty mike-mike was dangerously powerful to use on a light pickup. It must have been cradled in a soft mount that spread its recoil over a long cycle. The gunner was using the big weapon as a self-loader rather than trying to fire bursts of fully automatic fire.

The gunner was good—good enough that he slammed us with two of his next three shells. A chunk of our side armor fractured and bounced off the rear fender, leaving a hole for any further projectile to find.

I'd reloaded, but I didn't bother firing. I could spit in the gunner's direction and have as good a chance of hitting him as I would trying to shoot 600 yards with my low-powered grenade launcher.

A spark flicked from left to right across my vision and intersected with the Spike-K pickup. A white flash hid the cab momentarily; it had vanished before the *crack!* of the explosion reached my ears.

The four-by-four skidded sideways, then began to roll. A wheel flew off and bounced high in the air. The wreck bulldozed thirty feet through the scrub before the dust of its own destruction covered it.

We had a chance after all.

I wasn't sure but what the burst of 20mm shot hadn't wrecked the launching system on the police van as well as destroying the missiles mounted on it when the twin Gatlings opened fire. Somehow the Lynx had managed to reload. The deadliness of his aim with the laser-guided projectile was only to be expected—though it couldn't have come at a better time for me and Ditsy.

The TV truck bumped over the blast-scarred roadway where CHIEF hit the limousine with an anti-tank missile. We swayed around the curve in the highway just beyond. The night ahead of us ripped apart as the Spike-K pickups closed in around Wallace's car.

I flipped forward the half-inch-long lever projecting from the helmet over my left ear, switching the commo system from intercom to CB. I poked Channel 9 on the lighted keypad that was part of the bucket controls and shouted, "Lynx, this is Deadeye! Can you reprogram to home on a one-point-oh-six-micron targeting laser?"

Big Ben's vehicle was surrounded by Spike-K pickups in a loose ring, one or two hundred yards in radius. Kames' men popped up from irregularities in the terrain, fired a burst or a rocket, and skidded behind another hillock.

Wallace's hypervelocity missiles could open up any of the Spike-K vehicles—if they hit. The problem was that Big Ben couldn't see his opponents from his low-slung Grenadier limousine, except during the instant that one pickup or another lurched into sight, fired, and backed to cover again.

Spike-K gunners didn't have to search for their target. The limousine crawled down the road like a broken-backed snake. I could walk faster than the car's present rate of progress, but *any* movement was amazing.

Since I'd last seen the limousine, somebody'd shot through the right-front wheel guards and chewed the tire to rags. Even so, the massively-armored Grenadier managed to scrape along. Dust from bullet strikes puffed around the vehicle like surf hitting a rocky shore.

A four-by-four hid from Big Ben's missiles behind a stand

of box elders. Two ranch hands in the pickup's box were re-loading the recoilless rifle mounted on the roof of the cab. They saw us as soon as the TV truck lurched around the curve in the highway.

The 90mm recoilless had limited traverse. Its gunshield was no protection against us appearing unexpectedly from behind. One crewman tried to swing the recoilless to bear, while the other snatched an automatic rifle and blazed away. He must have loaded the whole magazine with tracers, because the rifle sprayed a single red streak toward the truck and me dangling high in the cherrypicker.

I emptied my clip as fast as my trigger finger would twitch. The last two tracers zipped to either side of the bucket. I think the fellow was just pointing his gun in a panic at the biggest target, the nose of the truck. Recoil lifted his muzzle high enough that the little bullets might have done some good.

None of my grenades hit where I was aiming. Since the four-by-four was only fifty yards away, I've shot better . . . but I won't claim the ranch hand was the only guy in a panic at the sudden meeting.

"Roger that, kid!" crackled the Lynx's voice over the CB. "Say when you've got a target!"

I was using dual-purpose rounds again. The shaped-charge warhead of my first grenade blew in the passenger-side window of the pickup's cab. The second hit the truck box, holing the thin armor but not doing a darn thing toward ending the fight.

My third grenade burst on the shield of the recoilless rifle. The gunshield was pretty thick, so I doubt the jet from my shaped charge penetrated—

But the sharp explosion startled the gunner into jerking his trigger while he and the other crewman were behind the breech of the recoilless rifle. The backblast was dangerous at a hundred feet. At twenty inches, it was a disaster. The yellow flare of powder gases burned the ranch hands to cinders and flung their corpses off the back of the vehicle.

"Kid!" shouted the marshal on my CB as I reloaded. "Give me a target!"

The 90mm's backblast seared the box elders and smashed the thinner stems to matchwood. Almost as an echo, a streak of light from the limousine spiked the four-by-four. The vehicle lurched and the right side of the cab—the side facing away from Big Ben's car—blew out in a spray of fragments. The *crack* of the projectile was as sharp and loud as that of a lightning bolt hitting twenty feet away.

Ditsy's father was desperate for a target. The streak of tracers had drawn his eye, a moment before the flare of the recoilless rifle stripped the copse which had concealed the pickup.

Big Ben's response was instant and dead on. His hypervelocity missiles relied on the kinetic energy of a tungsten penetrator rather than a high-explosive warhead for effect. One had shattered both doors of the Spike-K pickup like a bullet hitting china cups.

The raised cherrypicker gave me a panorama of the battle. I pointed my grenade launcher at a shelltopped vehicle in a gully on the far side of the ring. I hoped it was CHIEF, though I couldn't tell for sure at a range of 500 yards or more.

"Target, Lynx," I called as I touched the stud activating my weapon's ranging laser. "Target!"

The police van's missiles had a range of several miles, but they *weren't* fire-and-forget weapons. They had to be guided all the way to a target if they were going to hit anything beyond brush and dry grass.

Normally the operator focused on a target with the spotting head in the police van's turret. When the target was centered, the operator touched a button to stabilize the head and paint the target with a low-powered laser; then he launched a missile whose sensors homed on the reflected laser light. A few seconds after launch, the powerful warhead went off with a blast likely to destroy anything on four wheels as well as most larger vehicles.

But by the time the Lynx reloaded his turret, all the Spike-K pickups were out of sight of the van—except for the Tail-end Charlie shooting at me and Ditsy. The crippled van couldn't get close enough to help Big Ben as his limousine was shot to bits.

The police missiles were state of the art. The operator could reprogram their software to home on a wide variety of notches from the optical spectrum, chosen for atmospheric conditions and to avoid confusion with other laser equipment being used on a chaotic battlefield. Though the Lynx couldn't see the enemy himself, he could launch missiles and hand off their guidance to *my* ranging laser.

"Ditsy, stop us," I ordered. *I* didn't have triple-axis stabilizing gimbals to hold my invisible dot on the distant target, and the bucket was bobbing all over the map.

Ditsy kept driving forward. I'd forgotten my helmet was still switched to CB radio.

My target grunted up the side of the gully. I hadn't picked the right vehicle. This one was a four-by-four, not CHIEF, and it rippled a trio of 2.75-inch rockets from the rack on its shelltop.

One of them hit the limousine. From the size of the bang, the rocket carried the lighter ten-pound warhead rather than the heavy fourteen-pounder, but it was still enough to blow bits off the car.

Big Ben's missile pod rotated, but the four-by-four's driver simply clutched and let gravity roll the vehicle back out of sight.

Out of Big Ben's sight. *I* could see the pickup fine.

The laser-guided missile didn't need a flare pot for guidance. I didn't notice anything but a flicker of motion—

The flash of the missile warhead swelled like a pearl-white toadstool off the roof of the shelltop. Solid rocket fuel sprayed in a blazing fan over the ground behind the pickup, but the warheads that exploded did so individually instead of in a single sky-searing blast.

The four-by-four began to burn fiercely. A pair of reloads carried in the bed of the vehicle flew up in tight corkscrews which indicated damage to their folding fins.

I flipped the helmet lever back to intercom. "Ditsy," I said, "hold up and let me spot more targets."

We drew fire from a four-by-four whose driver either knew what I was doing or suspected that the TV truck mounted heavy artillery itself. The pickup rounded a grass hummock 200 yards from us. I saw the motion, but I was still searching for CHIEF and didn't pay any attention till the driver opened up.

The pickup mounted a three-barreled .50-caliber Gatling under the hood. The driver had maneuvered to bring his gun to bear. Ditsy was already braking in response to my order, so the initial burst streamed past the nose of our truck.

I turned to aim at the Spike-K vehicle. The ranch hand slewed his pickup expertly and hammered the front of the TV truck with his powerful machine gun. The red ribbon of his tracers wavered like the blade of a bandsaw, chopping and chewing at our windshield and bow. Bits of armor, tracer compound, and bullet jacket splashed in all directions. Fragments pinged against the bucket and needled my forearms. Our headlights burst in green flashes of tungsten.

The pickup lurched and exploded before I could fire at it. When the driver concentrated on us, he forgot to hide from the limousine. Big Ben skewered him with another hypervelocity missile.

The missile's track beyond the destroyed pickup glowed momentarily. Friction from the projectile had converted all solid matter in its direct path to gas.

Backblast marked a recoilless rifle firing at us from the left. The shell missed—high for the truck, low for me because it whapped the air inches beneath the arm of the cherrypicker.

"Ditsy, back up!" I shouted, hoping the headset was on intercom. The Lynx was probably crying for another target and the good Lord knew I wanted to give him one, but I had to survive the next Spike-K round.

I didn't see the shell burst next to a four-by-four advancing from the right in compound low to improve its position on the limousine. The pickup's crew knew they were taking fire, though. They answered it with a long burst from the 20mm cannon on the truck bed and the twin machine guns on the cab. They at least got the target's attention, because the gunner with the recoilless put his next round squarely on top of the right-hand pickup. Chunks of the vehicle and its crew went flying.

Two more four-by-fours targeted the one with the recoilless. I pronged one of them with my laser, flipped to CB, and called, "Target, Lynx!"

CHIEF's long 30mm gun slapped the night with a three-shot burst. Kames' personal vehicle was in a draw 300 yards away. The muzzle blast of the high-velocity gun sounded extremely loud because it was sharper than earlier gunfire.

The missile launcher on top of Big Ben's limousine was protected more heavily than the drivers of most cars were. That was how it had survived the battering thus far—and allowed Wallace to keep his enemies from closing in for the kill.

The launcher disintegrated under the triple hammer of Kames' shots. Blow-out panels on the top and sides failed as they were supposed to do. The yellow flash of exploding rocket fuel hid the limousine for an instant, but the blast did no real damage to the vehicle.

A second burst of 30mm fire shattered the limousine's windshield. It either killed the chauffeur or wrecked his controls, because the car wobbled off the road into a ditch.

Two four-by-fours blew up together. One was the vehicle well south along the highway, bobbing over my sights as it poured a stream of tracers across the Spike-K ring. A missile from the police van, unseen as the previous one had been, homed on my reflected ranging laser. The fierce white flash of the warhead was a half-second quicker than the *whop*. There was no secondary explosion, but ammo popped and rattled from the wrecked vehicle in a play of sparks like lights on a fountain.

I wasn't expecting the other explosion. It was really a series of three blasts, each louder than the one before. The pickup whose recoilless rifle had destroyed a friendly vehicle by mistake was now the mistaken victim of its two fellows—one the truck that the Lynx had just destroyed. The storm of autocannon and machine gun fire directed at the vehicle ignited ready munitions. An orange flash preceded each *whoomp* by a fraction of a second.

110

CHIEF was accelerating toward Big Ben's silent vehicle. Ditsy threw the TV truck into forward gear again. "No!" I cried—switched to intercom and repeated, "No, Ditsy! I'll spot—"

The 30mm gun cracked a full six-round clip into the limousine's broadside. Something that looked like a whole densely-armored door panel flipped into the air like a tiddly-wink.

"He's my father!" Ditsy shouted again.

The surviving Spike-K four-by-four opened up on us. The pickup mounted a 20mm cannon in the center of the hood and a rifle-caliber machine gun over either front fender. The weapons had some elevation and traverse, because the gunner on the passenger side managed to follow us pretty well as we drove toward the limousine on a course converging with that of the ranch hands' vehicle.

Shells and bullets whacked the side of the truck. Then the gunner noticed me, the first time anybody had tonight, and adjusted his fire upward. A double line of machine gun tracers and the great glowing balls of cannonshells clawed up through the night.

Ditsy was calling, "Daddy!" on the intercom. I knew Lynx Feldshuh wanted a target as bad as I wanted to give him one, but I didn't have *time*. I stroked my trigger, snap-shooting instead of bothering with the three-dot sights. Instinct was better than technology when the range was so short.

My first grenade missed. The cherrypicker arm rang like colliding trains when a pair of 20mm shells hit it, arm's length from my bucket. The four-by-four bounded toward us over a tussock, all wheels airborne.

I hit the corner of the driver's side window with my second shot. The armor didn't fail, but the flash/*bang!* startled

111

the driver. He jerked the steering wheel and got crossed up as he hit the ground again. The pickup rolled over sideways three or four times before coming to rest with its wheels spinning in the air.

CHIEF lay so close alongside the limousine that the muzzle of the 30mm gun almost touched its target. Everybody aboard the six-by-six noticed us coming at the same time. Kames clutched with a bang, reversing to get maneuvering room. The gun crew in the shelltop traversed their turret onto us, and the ranch hand riding shotgun with Kames rolled down his window and fired at me with a folding-stocked rifle.

I had one grenade left in the magazine. I lobbed it through the open window. A bright flash lit CHIEF's cab, but the thick armor retained all the blast and fragments.

Inside, with Stannard Kames.

The high-velocity autocannon fired three times. The muzzle blasts were so sharp that it felt as though someone was slapping my ears with a board. The TV truck's thick bow armor shattered at the point-blank impacts.

Then our ram plate hit CHIEF broadside.

I could look down at the six-by-six. The crash of the collision went on forever. The smooth, black vehicle lurched sideways, then over in a spray of gritty soil. It rolled completely. The shelltop separated from the crumpled pickup's bed and lay on the ground between us and CHIEF. Flames began to quiver in the cab.

The TV truck stalled and shuddered to a halt. At that point, the arm of the cherrypicker sheared off where the cannonshells had hit it. Inertia flung me and the bucket in separate arcs over the shuddering wreck of CHIEF.

The impact knocked all the breath out of me. I tried to get up. I couldn't, but my flailing hand found my grenade launcher. I clutched it to me, even though it was empty and I'd lost the bandolier of reloads somewhere.

I heard a voice whimpering. It was only later that I realized it was mine.

I saw headlights coming south on the highway. I still couldn't stand up, but I started to crawl toward the TV truck. The driver's door stood open. I heard Ditsy calling something as she reached through the limousine's shattered windshield.

I had to find ammo. . . .

A sedan skidded to a halt just in front of me. I aimed my empty grenade launcher at where the windshield ought to be.

The doors flew open. The Lynx had been driving. "What d'ye think you're doing, kid?" he snarled.

He'd taken the personal car of one of the warehousemen. Sheltered behind the other door, Hannah Martin scanned the terrain across the sights of a shoulder-fired rocket launcher.

I let my body go limp.

"Jesus," said the Lynx. Then he added, "Jesus *Christ*!" as he pounded across the pavement to the remains of Big Ben Wallace's limousine.

CHAPTER 11

The sound of machine guns firing brought me around.

I don't think I'd been unconscious, exactly, but my mind drifted in a gray limbo that was a long way away from the reality of the last—how long had it been? An hour, since the alarm sounded? Maybe even less.

The car the Lynx and Hannah commandeered carried twin machine guns on a roof mount above the passenger seat. The mount was fitted with a small Spalltex gunshield, but when the driver was alone, the guns fired forward—the amount of offset wasn't a serious problem.

The deputy marshal stood in the passenger compartment, looking out through the roof. She'd unlocked the ring. As my eyes opened, she triggered another short burst.

The paired lines of tracers arched northward at a 45° angle. They burned out just beyond the apex of their trajectory. Part of my mind wondered whether the spent bullets would fall on Mannheim, but I didn't have enough energy to feel upset at the possibility.

I got to my feet. My eyesight blurred, then became abnormally clear. From far in the distance, I heard a man cry, "For God's sake, help her!"

An automatic rifle fired straight into the air for emphasis. The shimmering muzzle flash marked a location half a mile back, where my WP grenade had cleared the bed of the pickup running parallel to us.

Someone else was screaming mindlessly from the same location.

Hannah Martin got out of the car.

"What's the matter?" the Lynx demanded from near the wrecked limousine. "Can't you shut him up?"

"It's all right," Hannah said as she walked over to him. "He's not doing any harm, shooting in the air. He won't take a hint from warning shots."

"Then finish him, woman!" snapped the marshal.

"At this range?" Hannah replied coolly. "All I'd do is start him spraying us for real—and maybe getting lucky. He'll keep, Lynx."

I joined them. Ditsy was there, too, squatting in the Grenadier's double-width rear doorway. Her father was out of his wheelchair and lying flat on the floor of the vehicle. She held his bandage-wrapped hand.

"Please . . . ," whimpered the man out in the darkness. "Help her!"

Big Ben groaned. I hadn't been sure he was still alive.

"When's the ambulance going to get here?" Ditsy demanded. Her voice had the timbre of a wheel bearing about to seize.

Marshal Feldshuh stepped aside and spoke into a cellular

phone. He was using an ear jack and a privacy screen over the mouthpiece, so I heard only murmurs and the hiss of a response.

He lowered the instrument. "They're already airborne, Miz Wallace," he said. "Wichita. It's not next door, but they'll be here soon."

Mecca Medical Center in Wichita was a long distance from Mannheim even by helicopter ambulance, but it was far and away the best hospital in the region. It made sense to send Big Ben there at once, rather than entrust him to lesser facilities and risk a transfer later. Money, after all, wasn't a problem—

But from the look of Big Ben's face in the faint moonlight, money might not be enough this time.

"Help . . . ."

"What's that?" I said. "Hannah."

The deputy and Marshal Feldshuh both looked around in surprise. They'd forgotten me in greater concerns.

I gestured with my grenade launcher toward the distant cries. Although the weapon weighed less than four pounds, I had to be very careful not to let it overbalance me.

Hannah shrugged. "Not our problem," she said.

She chuckled, a sound that reminded me of my brother in a way I didn't like. "I'd say it was Stannard Kames' problem," she added. "But I think he's in a higher order of trouble just now."

I couldn't possibly walk all the way to the crying ranch hand. I looked around for a vehicle.

The TV truck was nosed into the wreckage of CHIEF. The truck might be driveable—*might*—when the two were separated, but that was a job for a wrecker. The pickup that had been concealed in the box elders, though . . . that was just possible.

The Spike-K pickup was stalled within a hundred yards of the wrecked limo, but even that was almost too far for me. I began wobbling badly before I'd made it halfway. I found that if I gripped the grenade launcher with both hands, I could use it the way a tightrope walker uses a balance bar. Because I was so focused on reaching the vehicle, though, I didn't worry about what I was going to find when I got there.

The backblast by which the crew of the recoilless rifle killed themselves had done no damage whatever to the vehicle. Big Ben's hypervelocity missile would have gone through any part of the light pickup that it hit, including the engine. If I was lucky, when the projectile ripped into and out of the cab it had managed to miss all the important structures.

I was lucky.

The two ranch hands in the cab had been lucky too, in a manner of speaking. They'd died instantly.

The missile struck the driver's door, dishing the armor inward and punching a clean three-inch hole through the center of the panel. The projectile had started to wobble after the initial impact. The passenger door was gone, blasted across the scrub in hundreds of fragments.

Everything between the shoulders and hipbones of the two men in the cab was gone also.

I didn't let myself think about it. I pulled the remains of the bodies off the floor and seat buckets because I needed to make room. Then I climbed in from the passenger side and started the engine.

The bottom third of the steering wheel's circuit, between the spokes, was gone. The missile had clipped it as neatly as a custom shop could have done. Nothing else was damaged.

The controls worked fine, though the door panel bumped me in the side as I moved. I switched on the headlights and drove toward the cries and screams.

The smell inside the truck was worse than that of the rig I'd helped clean the day before. The missing door helped, but I couldn't roll down the window on my side.

On my way to where the wounded cowboys lay, I approached the upside-down remains of the truck they'd jumped from before it blew up. There wasn't much left. One rear wheel clung to the support frame, but everything else behind the cab had been blown away. The body I'd seen flop out when the door opened still lay within the wreckage.

He'd been trying to kill me.

My headlights fell squarely across the body. *She'd* been trying to kill me.

The crew from the bed of the pickup lay a hundred yards away, pretty much as they'd fallen: one alone, and the other two some ten yards south of him. One of the pair cradled the head of the other in his lap. He waved frantically at my headlights.

The cowboy's automatic rifle lay beside him. I thought there might be trouble when I got out and he realized I wasn't from the Spike-K, despite the vehicle. I'm not sure he even noticed.

"Fer God's sake, help me with Roxie," he begged in a cracking voice. "I try t' bandage her, but it burns through!"

My door was jammed. I climbed across the truck's console to get out. The victim was a woman. The fellow holding her had slit away the backs of her trouser legs; the edges of the cloth smoldered.

"Casey," she moaned. "Oh God, Casey, I hurt so bad. Help me—"

The moan rose to a shriek. *"—Casey!"*

I looked at her thighs. She'd caught most of the white phosphorus charge of my grenade. Bits of it still burrowed their way into her flesh. They wouldn't stop burning until they consumed themselves or they'd eaten completely through her.

I knew what we had to do. The torpor that had gripped me since I regained consciousness melted away in the heat of the woman's need.

"Can you help me with her, Casey?" I said as I bent down. I didn't know how badly *he* was hurt. "We'll carry her to the warehouse in the back of the pickup."

"I'm not Casey," the cowboy said. "I'm Frenchie Beaudean."

He glanced toward the third crewman. "He's Casey."

My eyes followed Beaudean's. I hadn't paid any attention to the silent man until that moment. He smiled when he saw me looking at him. His forehead glittered with sweat. A fragment, probably a long splinter of truck armor, had sawn away the lower half of his breastplate. There was a cavity where his belly should have been, gleaming with blood.

I looked away. "Help me with the woman!" I said harshly.

"C'mon, Roxie," Beaudean crooned. "You're going to be okay."

"God it hurts, Casey," she whimpered.

We walked her toward the back of the pickup. She was a dead weight, but she didn't fight us.

"We both l-like her, Casey 'n me," Beaudean said emotionlessly. "I th-thought she, she liked me better."

He climbed easily into the back of the truck. I wasn't sure I could have managed that, even though the tailgate had been removed for combat.

As I handed Roxie up to Beaudean, I saw that a boot lay on the bed of the pickup. I looked away as quickly as I could, but not before I saw that an inch of bone charred by the recoilless rifle's backblast protruded from the top of the footgear.

Casey closed his eyes. He began to keen, a high-pitched sound with edges like broken glass.

Beaudean stared down at the man on the ground. "B-buddy?" he said to me. "Will you—take care of Casey?"

I walked around to the open doorway. "Nothing to do about him," I said. The sound Casey was making sawed on my nerves.

"You know!" Beaudean said. "Put him—you know! Make him stop hurting, *please*!"

I got into the cab. I didn't answer.

I heard Beaudean crying as I backed up and started for Security Warehouse.

CHAPTER 12

knew what to do for white phosphorus burns because one hot day when we were alone at the shop, Erculo had taken off the shirt he normally wore. His chest was a mass of deep pits. I didn't say anything, but the way I looked aside after my first glance at the scarring was a question in itself.

As we worked, Erculo told me about the injuries and how he had survived them. His voice as he talked held no expression whatever . . . but it wasn't the sort of thing that I was ever going to forget.

In the rear of Security Warehouse were four bed-and-bath units for truck crews who were spending the night. The Fibrex blast that blew down the fence surrounding the complex had also left the broad driveway in front a tangle of wreckage. Chain-link fencing knotted around:

Poles shattered into jagged spears—

Bits of vehicle and weapons—

And bodies.

I drove straight through the wrack. There wasn't time to be delicate. Besides, the people who still lay on the ground were beyond pain, and that wasn't the case with Roxie in back of my truck. She'd begun to scream again.

There were several cars present that hadn't been in the lot when the alarm went off. Three uniformed warehousemen stared from the building's ruptured doorway as I arrived. The off-duty shifts had come in when the explosions roused them. They didn't try to stop me, which was good because Roxie's screams didn't leave me in much shape to discuss matters calmly.

The doors of the sleeping units were all ajar. I stopped in front of the first in line, hitting the brakes harder than I'd meant. Beaudean still wore his body armor. He slammed against the back of my cab, loud enough to sound like a projectile impact. I didn't even care.

"Get her in here fast!" I shouted as I climbed out of the truck. I thought of helping Beaudean, but it was more important to get water into the tub—if the units had tubs. If they didn't I was going to plug the drain of a shower stall and hope I could flood it to a sufficient depth.

There was a tub. I turned both taps full on. The temperature didn't matter near as much as filling the tub high enough to cover the phosphorus sizzling within Roxie's legs.

I met Beaudean in the doorway. He had the woman's arms crossed over his shoulders in a packstrap carry. She was still making sounds, but she hung as a dead weight. Her toes dragged behind him.

"Into the tub!" I said. I grabbed Roxie's legs and helped him wrestle her through the bathroom door. The light over the lavatory mirror gave me the first good look at her: brown hair with false highlights, vacant brown eyes, and roundish features that wouldn't have impressed me even if they hadn't been drawn white with agony.

Beaudean must see somebody else when he looked at her. There was as much pain on his face as there was in hers, but it wasn't physical with him.

We slid Roxie into the tub as the water ran. Beaudean supported her torso. The flecks of phosphorus stopped burning so long as they were underwater, but they'd reignite when air touched them again.

There was a first aid kit on the wall beside the lavatory mirror. I opened it and rummaged through to find the tweezers and a tube of antiseptic cream.

Roxie had fallen unconscious now that the pain no longer prodded her awake. Beaudean crooned to her. The tub was half full. Steam began to rise as water from the heater reached the faucet.

I reached past Beaudean and shut off the taps. The cowboy looked up in surprise.

"Turn her over," I ordered.

"Huh?"

I switched off the light over the mirror, then closed the door a crack so that only the faintest glimmer from the bedroom could enter. "Turn her over," I repeated. "We've got to get the bits out. Or they'll keep burning, buddy, they'll just keep right on burning."

"But—"

I'd been okay because I was taking things one after another in exact order. I hadn't realized how close to the surface my frustration was. Now I reached for the grenade launcher I'd leaned against the corner of the tub. The gun wasn't loaded, but a straight buttstroke into the cowboy's face would—

I froze. Beaudean was just as shook as I was, maybe more so. If it had been Ditsy there in the tub, moaning with holes burned halfway through her thighs . . .

"Here, I'll help you," I said as I knelt down. The mat was still folded over the edge of the tub. It was soaked. I slid it onto the floor. "We'll get the rest of the stuff out so we can bandage her. She's going to be all right, Frenchie."

Beaudean kept the woman's face from hitting the hard, extruded-plastic edge of the tub while I levered her legs around. I closed my eyes for a moment, then reopened them. I thought I might have to wait still longer, but then I began to make out glimmers like bits of rotting wood beneath the surface of the water. It was almost too faint to be real—

But as soon as the water drained away, every one of those shimmers would reignite into miniature flames and resume devouring Roxie's flesh.

I probed into the nearest wound with my tweezers. She shuddered. To do the job right, we ought to have a suction lift and a proper operating room, but this would have to be sufficient.

I brought up the tweezers. The tips glowed. I rubbed them clean on the wet bathmat, then reached in for more.

"Oh Casey," the woman whimpered. "I hurt so bad. . . ."

"She's going to be fine," I muttered.

There were twenty-seven separate bits on the backs of Roxie's thighs. I dipped matchhead-sized fragments of phosphorus out of every one of them. By the time I finished, the mat had dried enough that it was beginning to smolder. I gathered it up by the corners and carried it to the outside door of the unit.

Two warehousemen waited hesitantly beside the doorway. They looked embarrassed by the automatic rifles they carried, as if they hoped I wouldn't comment on the weapons. One of them was named Warsaw—Tom Warsaw, I thought. He lived a little ways up Liberty Street from our house.

"Ah, Mr. Deal?" he said. "Ah—we were wondering about, ah . . . who won?"

They were afraid that the Spike-K cowboys would return to make a clean sweep of anybody who worked for Big Ben Wallace . . . but mostly they were worried about their jobs. I thought of the sprawled bodies and felt dizzy with anger.

I flung the mat onto the concrete pad. "She didn't," I said. "Though I guess she'll live."

Warsaw cringed. "Please, fella," he said. "Is Mr. Wallace all right?"

I looked at him. It wasn't Tom Warsaw's fault that a woman's legs would be a mass of scar tissue for the rest of her life—or until she got reconstructive surgery that she'd never be able to afford. It wasn't the fault of anybody except the guy who'd sprayed her with white phosphorus.

Nobody's fault but mine.

"There's an ambulance coming, Tom," I said. "I figure he'll be okay. Ditsy wasn't hurt. She'll run things fine, you know her."

Ditsy. I needed to get back. . . .

I walked into the bathroom and switched the light on. Beaudean held the woman. She was silent again. "I'll help you get her onto the bed," I said. "There's cream for the, the hurt places."

Some of the pits were inches deep.

"Dry her off and keep her warm," I added as we lifted her, though Beaudean probably knew how to handle the treatment from here on out. "Or she'll, you know, die of shock."

I went back into the bathroom for my grenade launcher. As I left the bed-and-bath unit, Beaudean called, "Buddy? You saved her life. I'll never forget that."

Warsaw and his fellow had gone around to the front of the warehouse again. I thought of borrowing a car from one of them, but I didn't bother. The Spike-K pickup was good enough for the guy who'd burned a woman's legs half off.

On my way to the limo, I stopped where I'd picked up Roxie and Beaudean. I didn't see Casey. For a moment, a rush of thankfulness washed over me: somebody had come for him. He was no longer in pain, no longer my responsibility.

Then I noticed something in the grass. I let up on the clutch and turned the truck slightly to get a better view with my headlights.

Casey lay face down, a dozen feet from where I'd last seen him. He must have crawled there by himself. I don't know how he managed. A coil of intestine like a long pink worm marked his trail.

I swallowed, remembering Beaudean had asked me to put Casey out of his misery. He had to be dead now.

I drove on instead of getting out to check for a carotid pulse. Casey wasn't my responsibility if he was dead, and he *had* to be dead.

Vehicles were burning across a half-mile circuit of prairie. Ammunition cooked off. Small arms rattled a constant, spiteful background, punctuated at intervals by the shuddering blast of heavier munitions—rockets, mines, and recoilless-rifle shells.

A missile buzzsawed across the sky like a giant saffron pinwheel. The warhead detonated just before it hit at the far end of its arc. The flash sucked a ring of dust from the ground and lifted it toward the clouds, still expanding.

The underside of the ring flickered in subtle patterns from firelight and the snap of explosions. I was following it with my eyes when the car the marshals had borrowed put a burst over the cab of my pickup. The tracers snapped a foot or two above me, plenty close enough for a warning from 200 yards away.

I braked and took the truck out of gear. Lights winking in the northwest sky indicated the ambulance was on its way. I wasn't going to reach Big Ben—and Ditsy—before it landed if I tried to walk.

If my door would open, I might have flung off the side of the cab and waved, hoping they could recognize me through night sights. Now . . .

I flashed my headlights and drove on in creeper gear. If the marshals were going to kill me, they were going to kill me.

They didn't fire again. Either the marshals realized who I was, or they figured that starting a firefight now was the worst thing they could do with the medevac bird preparing to land.

When things settled down, I could have asked the Lynx or Hannah what their reasoning was. I didn't bother then, and now it's too late.

The borrowed car was empty when I parked beside it and got out. Marshal Feldshuh was talking on the cellular phone, while his deputy moved a pair of yellow light wands in slow arcs.

The helicopter ambulance hovered, a quarter mile out and a few hundred feet in the air. Ammo popping all around had made the pilot nervous. He knew that plenty of country boys can't resist the moving target that an aircraft provides, and there's a limit to how much armor you can hang on something that's got to be able to fly.

I walked over to the Grenadier. They'd somehow extended the wheelchair ramp, though it was gashed and wrinkled from punishment the limo had taken.

Ditsy straightened from where she sat beside her father and saw me. "Brian!" she shouted. "Where have you been?"

She was furious because I hadn't been exactly where she'd expected me to be. I thought about that. "I went for a drive," I said without inflection.

Moving around—doing something that *had* to be done—had been a good idea. I walked normally, now. The only problem was my hands. I'd scraped most of the skin off the heels of my palms when I skidded out of the cherrypicker. I'd been all right until I dipped them in warm water to pick the phosphorus out of Roxie. Since then my hands throbbed with every heartbeat. The pain was enough to give me vertigo.

"This isn't any time to fool around, Brian!" Ditsy said as she bent toward Big Ben again. "What if you'd missed the ambulance?"

"I'm not taking the ambulance," I said. I doubt she heard me. The medevac bird swept in at that moment and overwhelmed everything with the rushing hiss of its blades.

The helicopter's landing lights flooded us. Hannah Martin dropped her yellow wands on the ground and stepped back.

White-uniformed medics scuttled from the bird's open door, carrying a stretcher. They ducked instinctively, although the idling blades were high enough that they couldn't be reached even if the medics jumped with their arms outstretched.

The red-haired deputy touched Ditsy's shoulder and led her out of the way. As the medics loaded Big Ben, Hannah glanced at me in the glare of the landing lights. She lifted my right hand—I held the empty grenade launcher by my left fingertips—and examined the heel closely.

It wasn't pretty. I looked away. Hannah's touch felt cool and good.

Ditsy noticed what the deputy was staring at. She gasped. "Come *on*, Brian!" she said. The rotor blades grated her shout into thin syllables. She tugged me by the shirt-sleeve toward the ambulance.

I shook my head. "I'm all right," I said. I didn't try to make myself heard over the sound of the helicopter.

"Come on!" Ditsy repeated. "I'll pay for it! You need help!"

"You don't need me now," I muttered. I turned my back. I didn't have the energy to go far, but the motion pulled my sleeve out of Ditsy's grip.

After a few moments, the chopper's engine note rose. The blade-angle coarsened and the bird rose in a quick, slanting rush to swing westward again. We could hear the rotors throbbing for several minutes, but the impact of darkness when the landing lights switched off brought with it the feeling of sudden silence.

A few rounds of 20mm ammunition exploded in a farewell volley.

"I'll bandage your hands," Hannah Martin said.

"I'm all r—" I started to say. I caught myself. "Yeah," I said. "Thanks."

She had a first aid kit on her belt. I sat in the doorway of the borrowed sedan while she worked, quickly and efficiently, by the dome light's illumination.

The Lynx came over to us. He'd made a final pass over the Grenadier limousine, searching for anything that Big Ben wouldn't want him to have left. "We were right to run south," the old duelist muttered, as much to himself as to us. "I just hope Mr. Wallace sees it that way when he gets better."

"If he survives," the deputy said. She sealed a last bandage over the layer of antiseptic. The tight wrapping helped to contain the throbs.

"Aw, woman, don't be that way," the Lynx grumbled. "He'll be all right. When he thinks about it, he'll know that heading south was the only choice."

Hannah lifted my chin so that I met her eyes. "You haven't done a lot of dueling, have you, boy?" she said. "Brian."

"No, ma'am," I said. I twitched my fingers, to make sure they still moved—they did—and to give me an excuse for looking down at them.

"You'll get used to it," she said. "After a while, it won't bother you at all. Remember, they were trying to kill you too."

"Yeah, just a buncha thugs," said the Lynx gruffly. "Say, you did a good job, kid. A great job. It would have been a whole lot harder without you helping."

I didn't respond. "Lynx," Hannah Martin said coldly. "Cut the crap, all right? He was *here* while we were still stuck a mile away."

The Lynx looked off into the distance as though he hadn't

heard. "There's nothing more we can do here," he said. "We'd better get back and make sure the warehouse is secure."

"Can you give me a ride home?" I asked, looking at my hands. I tried to stand up. A back spasm caught me when I was half way. Hannah grabbed me to keep me from falling.

Marshal Feldshuh looked at me. "Can't you drive?" he said in surprise. "Hell, kid—take the truck you were futzing around in. I figure you're owed your pick of the salvage for helping. For what you did tonight, I mean."

I thought of the cab of the pickup, splashed with blood and other fluids. I'd used it because I had to, but now—

I pulled away from the deputy's hands. "That's okay," I said. "I'll walk."

"No," said Hannah Martin. "We'll give you a lift. And we'll do it now, before we worry about the warehouse that's as secure now as it ever was since Big Ben built it. Right, Lynx?"

The Lynx looked at her and grimaced. "C'mon," he muttered as he stumped around to the driver's side of the car. "I just hope Mr. Wallace understands that south was the only choice. . . ."

CHAPTER 13

It was midmorning before I started walking to work. I ached all over, especially my hands, my ribs, and the scabs on my knees when my legs swung. I'd gotten scraped up pretty good when I came out of the bucket.

Our wrecker, towing a pickup gutted by one of Big Ben's missiles, passed me as I walked along. The driver was a fellow named Mickey somebodyorother. He worked for Joe Ezelle, who ran the repair shop in Cross Creek.

Mickey didn't stop or even wave. Maybe he didn't recognize me. Well, that was all right. I didn't have a lot of use for Mickey—nor his boss, truth to tell. The work they did in Cross Creek wasn't a patch on Erculo's.

There were near a hundred people crowding the yard of Erculo's shop. Cars parked up and down the highway, besides filling the K660 lot across the road. It scared me to see.

The tow truck was caught in the crowd. Mickey laid on

his horn, but people were more interested in looking over the shot-up four-by-four than they were in getting out of his way. Millie Spence, who must've been sixty, stuck her arm all the way through the entrance hole in the driver's side door, cackling to a pair of friends as old as she was.

I wondered whether anybody'd gotten around to removing the bodies of the crew from the cab—and whether Millie knew or cared.

I figured I'd have to fight my way through the mob to find Erculo and apologize for being late. I wasn't in shape for it, my body nor—whatever you want to call the rest of me, mind or soul or spirit, not that either.

To my surprise, Butch Franklyn saw me and shouted, "Hey, lookee, it's Deadeye! How're ye doing, Deadeye?"

He was serious. He came at me with his arm outstretched to pump my hand. I tried to shift my grenade launcher from my right hand to the left. The muscles over my ribs were too sore and I wound up with the gun slanted over my chest like I was holding it at port arms and half threatening.

I got flustered. Butch jumped back like he'd seen Hell gape for him. "Sorry, Mr. Deal!" he gasped. "Sorry, I didn't mean t' presume, *sorry.*"

"I just want to get to work," I muttered. I wondered why I was even carrying the grenade launcher, because I sure God didn't want ever to use it again. I remembered the look on Stannard Kames' face, lighted by the explosion of the round I'd fired into CHIEF's cab.

Folks backed away, opening a corridor. They stared at me, people I'd known the last twelve years of my life, but these weren't the expressions I'd ever seen on their faces before.

I thought of how they'd looked at JC after the firefight

133

north on the highway. Right then I'd have run away if I hadn't needed to see Erculo.

"Don't you have homes?" I muttered as I shrugged past them. I kept my eyes on the graveled lot. Work boots, casual shoes, and the cuffs of dungarees shuffled back from me. "Don't you have *homes*?"

Erculo's lockup was full already. I didn't know why Mickey was hauling another wreck into the lot like this. I looked up at the tow truck's cab as I passed and said, "Mickey! Take it around behind. When you get all of them together, we'll run a bale of concertina wire around them for security till the owners pick them up."

"Hey, who died and made *you* God?" Mickey called down angrily.

Mickey could do what he pleased. I walked on, not bothering to answer. I remembered JC's comment about slanging matches with punks. . . .

I glanced back over my shoulder, not thinking what I was doing, but my eyes measured the angle to the wrecker's open side-window. I didn't say anything, I didn't do anything, I didn't *mean* to do anything.

Mickey stalled the tow truck. He ducked down behind the dash. The window slammed closed.

I didn't mean to do *anything*.

It struck me that there might not be anybody to claim the Spike-K vehicles. Stannard Kames didn't have any relations that I'd heard of, and there couldn't be many of his crew alive after last night's battle. Some long-haul truckers. The cowboy who'd driven the half-track, I supposed—unless the Lynx had nailed it for good measure while Ditsy and I were out of sight of the van. . . .

I couldn't believe how many people had died. I just couldn't believe it.

The police van was too big to fit into the shop's internal bay, so Erculo was replacing its back wheels on the outside hoist and platform. All four wheels were gone, and I don't mean just the tires.

That wasn't the disaster it would have been with most vehicles. The van was expected to take serious damage and engineered so that repairs were as simple as possible. All six wheels, their mountings, and the bevel gears driving them were identical and easy to reach. The Fibrex explosion might have torqued the frame, but there was nothing that the shop's equipment couldn't handle.

Joe Ezelle held a driveshaft in a flexible powerhead while Erculo guided the part into place under the van. He was a big, soft-looking man. He wore his black hair in a long ponytail, but he was noticeably balding on top.

"A little farther," Erculo called. "No, no! A little! Back it off and—"

He skidded his dolly out into daylight. "Look, I'll take the powerhead and you—"

"I'll do it, sir," I said. I nodded apologetically to Joe and added, "I'm used to our equipment."

Erculo shaded his eyes with his hand and scrambled to his feet. "Brian!" he said. "What are you doing here?"

"I—" I blurted. "Sir, I'm sorry I'm late."

Erculo wouldn't fire me for being two hours late—would he? Though with the amount of work the shop had, and him needing to call in help from Cross Creek to handle it . . .

"Sir, I disconnected the phone," I said, looking at my hands. They were bandaged where I'd scraped the heels when

I hit. "I'm sorry, I shouldn't have done that, but it kept ring-ing and I didn't want to talk to anybody. . . ."

I'd started to unplug the phone jack. Mom had grabbed me and cried, "No, no! It may be John calling me for help!"

I smashed the phone with the butt of my grenade launcher. I hit it three or four times, sending bits of plastic and silicon sailing across the kitchen. I expected Mom to say something, but she just went to her bedroom and closed the door.

"What?" said Erculo. "No, I mean, I thought you were in the hospital. The helicopter took you off with Mr. Wallace, surely?"

Joe Ezelle looked at me like I was a two-headed calf. His eyes made me feel itchy, worse than I did already.

"No sir," I said to Erculo, pretending that Ezelle and the hundred other people behind me didn't exist. "Ditsy wanted me to go—"

I thought about the night before. I had to swallow before I could go on.

"—but I was okay. And I knew you'd need help today with the, the . . ."

I waved my hand from the wrist only, toward the police van. "And the rest."

If I'd gone off to a hospital with nothing to do but think about the past, I'd be going crazy for sure. I had to do some-thing I understood.

I hadn't gotten to sleep till dawn. The pain whichever way I lay was part of the problem. Mostly, though . . . so long as it was dark, I saw dead men's faces when I closed my eyes.

Erculo looked at me. I think he understood, because he said, "Yes, that's right, Brian. I do need you this morning."

"I told Mickey to start a cache in the back of the lockup," I said in relief. "I can go get wire from the hardware store to secure it while you and, and Mr. Ezelle are working here."

"Yes, that's—" Erculo began. As he spoke, he looked up and saw our tow truck still mired in the crowd at the entrance to the lot.

"What's he doing that for?" Erculo snapped. "Can't he see there's too much in here already? You there! Take that around behind, where there's room. And then drag out these others that you've stowed here!"

Mickey had dropped two wrecks in front of the lockup's gate, I guess while Erculo's vision was blocked by the police van. One was a pickup, about six inches lower than it'd been before it rolled. I walked over and fingered the wreck's scarred side window.

Muzzle blasts had blackened and rippled the paint on the hood in front of the cannon port. I remembered white flashes in the corner of my eye as I squeezed my trigger and 20mm shells cracked toward me along the cherrypicker arm.

"Look, I'm trying to back up, ain't I?" Mickey whined.

"How was he supposed to know where you wanted the overflow, Herk?" Ezelle complained.

Erculo glanced at the Cross Creek mechanic. I hoped his face never set that way when he looked at me. "Joe," he said, "help your man tow in the rest of the debris, if you will."

"What?" said Ezelle. "You need me here!"

"Brian will be sufficient," my boss said coldly. "As he pointed out, he knows the equipment."

"Don't be a bloody fool!" Ezelle snarled. "You don't want a boy working on a job this important!"

"The window, Brian," Erculo said. "That's where your grenade hit?"

"Yessir," I said.

I wondered why the window hadn't blown out. The Spalltex wasn't unusually thick. Just the angle or my bad luck, I supposed. Not that I could complain about luck.

"According to Deputy Marshal Martin," Erculo said with cold formality, "Brian dealt with most of the other ranch vehicles as well. Mr. Ezelle, I offered to pay for your help. If you don't choose to provide the help *I* require, then take yourself and your *boy* off my property."

Joe Ezelle blinked. "Hey, Herk," he said. "You know I didn't mean nothing." He charged into the crowd, shouting, "Hey you people! Get your asses out of the way so we can get these wrecks moved, you hear me?"

Erculo lay down on his dolly again and slid under the van. I took over the powerhead. I found that if I concentrated on the job, I could almost forget the hundreds of eyes staring at my back.

We got the drivetrain repaired in less than an hour. Every once in a while Erculo glanced at where blood was starting to leak through the bandages on my hands, but he didn't say anything.

I was glad of that. Using my hands didn't hurt. Not worse than they hurt to begin with, anyhow.

When we got the van drivable again, we started in on the armor. Every panel on the right side of the vehicle had to go. Armor-piercing shot from the twin Gatlings had chewed a long snake-pattern across the flank and rear.

A couple places it looked like there'd been penetration, but that could've been just chunks spalled off the back side of the plating rather than projectiles entering. We'd worry about internal damage after we got the body shell back to spec.

Like the running gear, the police van's armor was built from standard modules—mostly heavy plates normally used on tractor cabs. Even so, we would have run through our stock before finishing the job except that Erculo remembered the rig hijacked two days before. The four-inch side plates were undamaged.

We robbed two of them from the wreck and fitted them onto the back of the police van. If Stannard Kames' heirs complained, Erculo could pay them at leisure. Until the Lynx was sure all the dust had settled from the battle the night before, he wasn't a bit interested in having his van out of action.

The crowd in the work area thinned when Joe and Mickey towed fresh wrecks out behind the shop. There wasn't much entertainment in watching a couple guys work. Much better to point at the damage, and laugh, and tell your girl and your buddies what you would've done if it'd been you there . . .

I wished to God that it had been somebody else there. But it was me, and in my memory it would be me for however long I lived.

Hannah Martin drove up on her trike just after lunch. She'd mounted a single hypervelocity rocket over each back fender. To aim, Hannah had to point the trike toward the target circle on her windshield heads-up display. It was an agile machine that dialed lean angles into all three wheels to compensate for centrifugal force on tight turns.

I didn't doubt the deputy marshal's ability to put rounds exactly where she wanted them. Seeing Big Ben turn pickups inside out with similar weapons had made me a believer in the effectiveness of hypervelocity missiles.

Though Hannah managed to look comfortable no matter what she had on, the first thing she did after pulling into the yard was to take off her gauntlets, her helmet, and her massive back-and-breast clamshell. Underneath the body armor, she wore a tank top whose thin mesh fluoresced wildly when sunlight struck it. The fabric was perfectly transparent in the shade.

Erculo stuck his head around the back of the police van to check the new arrival. "Coming to see how we're getting on?" he called to the deputy marshal. He smiled tightly, proud of the progress we'd made.

"No," Hannah said. "I just came to pick up something I left last . . ."

She paused, staring at the van. She teased her coppery hair looser with her left hand. "But you do have it fixed, don't you?" she said. "This quickly?"

Erculo's smile gained another thousand candlepower. "Two more studs on the last plate," he said. "The rotating head of the missile launcher, that will have to be replaced, and we won't have the part for two days, maybe a week."

"It worked last night," Hannah said with a frown.

Erculo nodded. "It works now, but the cover plate has a deep chip out of it and should be replaced." The smile grew brighter yet. "And the van must be painted, of course."

The plates of armor we'd just attached were mostly in primer gray, but the shade varied by manufacturer and production lot. The combination gave the side of the police van a blotchy, camouflaged look. The back was similar, except that the two pieces we cannibalized from the Spike-K tractor were painted electric blue.

The deputy marshal unlatched the side door of the van and tugged it open. The armored panel rolled easily on its track. In the center of the van was a console from which an operator could direct any or all of the vehicle's weapons systems. There was an identical set for the driver, but while the van was moving he would have his hands too full for accuracy with anything but the forward-firing armament.

Semicircular guards of tubing reached eighteen inches down from both turret rings. They protected manual controls fitted so that the van's crew could use its weapons even if the vehicle lost all power.

Hannah Martin stepped into the van. "I'm not the sort who confuses looks with performance, Erculo," she said. The multicolored serape JC had given her was draped over the back of the console's seat. She picked it up and added, "The Lynx isn't either, though he *does* like to look."

She grinned at me, then gave her torso a little shimmy. I swallowed and went to the back of the van again. I needed to finish tack-welding the tenons which held the armor in place on the studs.

"Not much like his brother, is he?" Hannah said in a throaty voice. Erculo answered, but I drowned the words in the buzz of my welder.

THE SQUARE DEAL slid into the lot with no sound but the crunch of gravel beneath its tires. I locked the welding head back into its bracket in the mobile work bench and wiped my hands on my shop apron as I walked out to greet my brother.

CHAPTER 14

JC's arrival brought the crowd oozing around to the front of the shop again, even though Joe Ezelle and Mickey were pulling in from the south with another pickup. This one was the six-by-six I'd hit just before the main battle started.

JC stood for a moment on his door coaming to gain six inches of height and a better view of the wreck being towed. Stretching made him look even more like a lithe, powerful cat. I couldn't imagine that a man with the background JC seemed to have didn't wear body armor, but there wasn't any sign of its weight or stiffness when he moved.

JC whistled as he hopped down and shook my hand. "Your work, Brian?" he asked, gesturing toward the six-by-six with his left thumb.

The last I'd seen of the six-by-six was a blur as it rolled, overprinted by images of the flash that had destroyed it. I'd been too busy with the rest of the battle to stare at any vehicle that was out of action.

Now I looked. The fourteen rockets ready in their launchers had exploded, flattening the shelltop and ripping the roof off the pickup's cab. The reloads in the truck bed hadn't detonated, but they'd burned. The metal parts of the pickup's frame and drivetrain stuck out at odd angles from a mass of armor melted liked taffy by the intense heat.

"Yessir," I said. "Yes, JC. I did it."

"Well, I'll tell the world!" JC chuckled. "You're the class act of the Deal family."

He sounded half like he meant it . . . but what I saw in my brother's eyes was very like the expression when he looked over Terry and the Pirates moments before he killed them all.

"Good afternoon, Mr. Deal," said Hannah Martin. "Or would you prefer that I call you 'JC'? I came to pick up your gift . . . since I didn't think the van's repairs would be finished before the next time I felt cold."

JC looked the police vehicle up and down. Though we'd replaced the damaged panels, the extent of those replacements indicated the degree of pasting the van had taken the night before.

"You were in the thick of it too, I see, Deputy," my brother said. His grin broadened without growing noticeably warmer. "Or whatever *you* would prefer to be called."

Hannah Martin turned her head. "Erculo?" she asked. "Is there any reason I shouldn't take the van out?"

"Not yet, lady," Erculo answered with a shake of his head. "We haven't test-driven her yet. Brian, why don't you—"

Hannah gave a brief, dismissive stroke with her hand. "No need," she said. "You have work to do. Mr. Deal and

I will take her for a drive . . . and maybe we can discuss pet names, while we're at it.''

She had been standing in full sunlight as she spoke. Now she extended her arm holding the serape to shade but not conceal her bosom. Her smile was as hard and challenging as JC's own.

"Come, lad," Erculo said in a clipped voice. "We'll inventory the damage to Miss Wallace's truck, next.''

"JC?" I said. "I was wondering?''

My brother slammed the van's sliding door, then opened the passenger-side door and gestured Hannah inside with a short bow. He turned to me and raised an eyebrow. "Yes?" he asked.

"I was wondering how you knew about the fight last night," I said. "Since you were up north?''

JC closed the hinged door with the thump*clack* that proved we'd aligned the new portal correctly when we mounted it. Automatic deadbolts locked the van's door whenever it was closed, to prevent it from springing open in action—and leaving the crew vulnerable to everything from derringer bullets on up.

"Indeed I was up north, brother dear," JC said. He walked around the bow of the van to the driver's side. "And I stopped in Chalybeate Springs to recharge. The trucking company there has a mast high enough to pull in CB signals from a hundred miles in any direction, and they were all talking about the gunfight in Mannheim.''

JC's smile was like a gunport unmasking. "More like a war, they said. Does that satisfy you, Brian?''

I lowered my eyes. "I'm sorry, JC," I said. Watching Hannah take my brother into the van that way made me feel,

I don't know, sick and angry, I guess. "I didn't think about it being news. I guess it was."

"News indeed," JC agreed with a nod. "Or would have been if you'd filmed it, which I dare say you were too busy to do."

He laughed cheerfully and glanced toward the tow-in cache again. "I'm sorry to have missed that one, to tell the truth. To watch, I mean. You obviously didn't need any help."

He got into the driver's seat of the van. After a moment's fumbling with unfamiliar controls, all the windows polarized into mirrors.

JC's voice came from the roof speaker, saying, "By the way, ladies and gentlemen . . . I'm sure none of you would presume to touch my car while I'm away—but it might be as well to mention that that would be a *very* bad idea. Depending on how I've left the system, either an alarm goes off—or THE SQUARE DEAL discharges a white phosphorus grenade toward the side the touch came from. We wouldn't want that."

The loudspeaker cut off, clipping the last of Hannah Martin's throaty chuckle. The van, scarred but perfectly functional, pulled out through the crowd that parted for it.

"The TV truck," Erculo repeated mildly.

"Yessir," I said. I went to bring it around to the external bay. Folks had mostly scattered when JC mentioned Willie Pete. A few hung on, staring at THE SQUARE DEAL like the sedan was a loose cobra. I knew my brother might be bluffing, but I wouldn't want to bet on that myself.

The TV truck was a worse job than the police van had been. There were three manufacturers involved—Ital did the chassis, but the coachwork was custom, and a separate custom builder was responsible for the specialty TV equipment, including the cherrypicker.

145

None of the three of them had been in the least concerned about repairs, which was the way it usually went. Erculo had told me that the first day I came to work for him, and the police van was the only exception I'd run into since.

Besides that, we'd taken fire from all four sides. A pair of good-sized shells had penetrated from the left, staring fires. The automatic extinguisher system had quenched them, but the blasts of chemical foam had done damage of their own.

CHIEF had fired tungsten penetrators, not high-explosive shells. The last three point-blank rounds pierced our truck from bow to the heavy plates covering the stern—partly, I suppose, because of the way light- and medium-caliber weapons had worked over the front before CHIEF started firing. The whole windshield was crazed into patterns that scattered light like a diffraction grating. I don't know how Ditsy had been able to see to drive.

CHIEF's 30mm shots penetrated the windshield at chest height. One round had carried away an edge of the driver's seatback.

I had to look away when I saw that. The shells flying at *me* hadn't been frightening: I'd been too busy answering them whatever way I could. Having the leisure to see what had almost happened to Ditsy made my stomach turn. I wasn't angry at her anymore.

I didn't hear a car arrive, but onlookers calling ''Howdy, Miz Wallace,'' brought my head out of the truck cab. Ditsy was getting out of her personal vehicle, a dune buggy she'd named PRINCESS, with heavy muffling over the motor and drivetrain. A lot of off-road vehicles were configured to make the most noise their drivers could wring out of them. The loudest thing about PRINCESS was the grunch of her tires.

Those tires were run-while-flat models whose woven core

maintained the equivalent of 10 psi pressure even if the tires had been shot to bits. PRINCESS wasn't fast. Her armor wouldn't stop more than a pistol bullet on a good day, and the 2.75-inch rocket on either flank was more cosmetic than a threat beyond point-blank range. The rockets didn't have any aiming apparatus beyond a reflector ring on the windshield.

On the other hand, the dune buggy would go just about anywhere—including up a 60° grade—without fuss or bother. That made PRINCESS the perfect vehicle for Ditsy.

"Brian?" Ditsy called. "Can I talk to you?" She looked over her shoulder at the crowd clinging like moss to tree bark, waiting for a dollop of vicarious excitement. "In private?"

"Use the studio in the back of your truck here, Miss Wallace," Erculo called from under the vehicle, where he was checking the running gear. "It's soundproof."

To my surprise after I crawled back through the wreckage of the cherrypicker's drive unit, the studio was almost undamaged. CHIEF's penetrators had punched a trio of clean holes, but the bursts of automatic fire that I remembered hitting our rear quarters hadn't gotten through the armor. I could cuss the vehicle from a repair standpoint, but the builders hadn't skimped on protection.

Ditsy slammed the studio's outside entrance on the people pressing after her to ask questions. She leaned her shoulders against the door and shuddered. "I never thought I'd be the one being chased," she muttered with her eyes closed.

"I didn't expect to see you," I said. The air in the studio was hot with the air conditioning off, and there was a burned tinge to it. "Is your dad all right?"

"He's resting easily!" Ditsy snapped. Her eyes opened and her face knitted in contrition. "Oh, I'm sorry, Brian. It's just—I mean, I must have said that a hundred times already. Because it's all the doctors would tell *me*. And it doesn't mean anything!''

"It means he's not dead," I said. "Which means he's lucky. Luckier than Stannard Kames.''

"He wasn't hit directly," Ditsy said in a low voice. Her eyes looked through me, deep into the events of the previous night. "But fragments of the armor cut him, his face, all over. He looks as though a cat was playing with him, a big cat.''

I reached for her. She came willingly, but only for a moment. Then she squeezed me and stepped back.

"He's in good hands," Ditsy said without inflection.

"The best," I agreed.

"Anyway," she went on, "that's not why I came. There wasn't any point in me staying in Wichita when, when there was nothing for me to do there. I want to learn who was behind it. And to stop them before they do it again.''

I shook my head. Maybe the burned smell was making me dizzy. I wondered what it came from. . . .

"I don't understand, Ditsy," I said. "The Spike K did it. Heck, Stannard Kames himself did it. And he *won't* be doing it again.''

"No, you're wrong," Ditsy said, not angry, but not interested in an argument either. She shook her head, making the long ruff of her hair undulate beneath the helmet she wore. "I don't—''

She paused, then tried again. "I don't regret—''

She shook her head violently. Her eyes were closed. I remembered that she must have been looking into CHIEF's cab also when my grenade went off. Maybe the distortion of the battered windshield had concealed from her the look on Stannard Kames' face when he died . . . but maybe not.

148

"Stannard Kames got exactly what he deserved," Ditsy said, enunciating carefully. "I don't . . . regret that. But he wasn't behind the trouble. That was somebody else."

"I'm listening," I said. The Spike-K Ranch had come loaded for bear. They'd had every intention of getting the Lynx out of the way and killing Big Ben. That was as simple as it came.

"Kames arrived looking for contraband," Ditsy said.

"Well, sure, he had to say something," I said.

"Don't interrupt!" Ditsy snapped. I might have backed her in a major firefight—saved her *father's* life besides—but that didn't give me the right to make silly noises when I ought to be listening to what she had to say.

"Kames was looking for contraband," she went on when she was sure I'd been stepped on properly. "And he found it. Twelve cases of ammunition in our warehouse had the same lot numbers as the cargo stolen from the Spike-K rig hijacked two nights ago. That's not a coincidence."

Ditsy nodded her chin briefly, indicating it was my turn to talk—if I had anything useful to say.

I cleared my throat. "Planted?" I suggested. "They had time. . . ."

I let my voice trail off. Kames and his ranch hands *didn't* have time to plant the loot, not twelve cases of it and not without the warehouse staff seeing what was going on. Like enough, both of Wallace's night men had survived the shooting. Certainly the Spike-K crews hadn't specifically targeted the warehousemen to shut them up.

"No," Ditsy said flatly. "Besides, that ammunition—six of seven-point-six-two, two cal fifty, and the rest twenty-millimeter—corresponds to the twelve-case lot delivered to the warehouse yesterday morning. I didn't have anything else to do on the flight back from Wichita, so I checked that with my cellular modem."

She ticked her chin down. I didn't say anything.

"Stannard Kames may have honestly believed my Dad was knowingly receiving stolen Spike-K goods to get back at him," Ditsy continued after a moment. "*I* don't believe that."

Boy, was I glad I'd kept my mouth shut!

"*I* believe that Davidson and Sheen delivered that hijacked ammunition to our warehouse in the shipment yesterday morning," Ditsy said. "And I'll bet that Kames was tipped off to find it there, too."

"By somebody who had it in for your dad?" I asked. That would cover most of the folks in Mannheim, one way or the other; though I didn't guess anybody in town hated Big Ben worse that Stannard Kames did. It seemed from what Ditsy was saying that even Kames had taken a real prodding to get him to move.

"By somebody who wanted Marshal Feldshuh and as many of the Spike-K gunmen as possible out of the way," Ditsy explained. "Even if they didn't expect a clean sweep, they must have known that the marshal and Daddy between them were going to account for a lot of Stannard Kames' thugs, wouldn't they?"

I nodded. With two men hating each other the way Kames and Big Ben did, it was going to be war to the knife when they finally mixed it. Numbers were on the Spike-K side, but Big Ben was driving top-grade equipment and backed by the Lynx and Hannah Martin.

"I don't like Stannard Kames—" Ditsy went on.

Didn't like, I thought. I didn't speak aloud.

"—but his people patrolled a wide range. If they found a bike gang had taken up residence in territory they thought the Spike-K owned, they were going to do something about it.''

I nodded.

''And the Lynx,'' I said, ''is the only local law around here that anybody'd worry about. Cross Creek and Welborn, they've got citizen posses, but they're not going to go out of their way to find trouble.''

''I want to go to Chalybeate Springs tonight,'' Ditsy said. ''Secretly. I want to see just what kind of an operation Davidson and Sheen is, and I want to see if any other operation is going on there.''

She tossed her head. ''Will you go with me, Brian?'' she asked.

I began to finger one of the 30mm holes in order not to have to look Ditsy in the face. Soundproofing foam had melted and bubbled from the shot's friction. ''Ditsy,'' I said, ''that's a job for—''

''If you're worried about your job,'' she broke in, ''don't be. I'll clear it with Erculo. Remember, Brian, *I'm* Wallace Enterprises now, until Daddy gets out of the hospital.''

''I don't mean that,'' I said, forcing myself to meet Ditsy's flashing black eyes. ''I mean it's a job for the Lynx, not you.''

Ditsy shook her head dismissively. ''Lincoln Feldshuh is a gunman,'' she said crisply. ''That's what he was hired to be. He doesn't know anything about an investigation. Or do you think I ought to contact the state police?''

I snorted. Us folks in the Central Prairies, we pretty much take care of our own. Partly, that's because we don't much like outsiders; but it's also true that none of the ''higher authorities'' have ever shown much inclination to give us a hand.

"Brian," Ditsy said, "I'm going to Chalybeate Springs tonight. I'm a reporter, it's my job, and—" Her voice started to break. She caught it. There were tears in the corners of her eyes as she continued, "And it was my *father* they did this to. They're going to pay for that, whoever they are!"

"All right, Ditsy," I said. "If you're going, I'll go with you. But I don't think it's a good idea."

Her face lost all its fierceness. "Thank you, Brian," she said. "Without you last night, we'd all have been killed."

She kissed me. I was so surprised that I didn't get my arms around her before she'd drawn back and opened the studio door. I guess the folks staring at us thought that I was blinking because the sunlight hit me in the face.

Lynx Feldshuh pulled up beside PRINCESS as Ditsy and I stepped out of the studio. The marshal's personal transportation was a massively armored sedan, a no-frills vehicle built by Magnum for the courier trade. For all the car's lack of flash, its protection was on a level with that of THE SQUARE DEAL.

The missile launcher on the roof was heavily armored as well. The missiles were held in a rotary launcher and fired through a single port, so they didn't have ripple capability. Neither were they as vulnerable as the normal, podded arrangement.

Lincoln Feldshuh had stayed alive for a long time by remembering that duelists—and lawmen—made a lot of enemies, some of whom were more interested in a sure kill than a fair kill. Because of that, he drove a sedan that could be expected to survive a bushwhacker's first shot and leave the Lynx able to reply with skills honed by years of demolishing his opponents.

As the marshal got out of his car, he eyed PRINCESS and

THE SQUARE DEAL with an identical lack of expression. When he saw Ditsy leaving the TV truck, his face brightened into what I realized was a professional smile. Dorothea Wallace was no longer just the boss's daughter; she was in charge. You could make a case—Big Ben probably would have said so—that the Lynx had screwed up bad the night before, and that was why Big Ben was "resting easily."

Now he took off his helmet respectfully and said, "Miz Wallace," with a little nod. "I was just checking progress on the van. Until we get back, I'll be patrolling in LIZZIE, there—"

He gestured toward his sedan. It was painted a nondescript green, without a name or other markings.

"—but it's not the same if there's serious trouble again, you know."

"Hannah took it out for a test drive," I said quickly, before somebody else said the wrong thing. "We got it back in shape except for cosmetics, though it'll look funny till we get around to painting it."

"Your deppity took JC Deal out for a test drive, Marshal," Chick Wilson called from the crowd. He smacked his lips. "*In* the van."

"*Recreation* vehicle, I reckon you could call it," said somebody I didn't see.

The Lynx looked about as mad as I've ever seen a human being, but the first thing he did was settle his helmet carefully on his head. Then he checked the slip of his holstered sidearm, a heavy pistol with a folding fore-grip and three-round burst capacity.

"When did they leave?" he asked. His voice was so hoarse that I wouldn't have understood the words if I hadn't been watching him as he spoke.

"I believe they're returning now, Marshal Feldshuh," Ditsy announced in clear, precise tones that reminded everyone that she spoke for Wallace Enterprises. "No doubt you will go your way, and Brian's brother will go his—without difficulty."

The police van rolled south down State 149 at a sedate pace. Hannah Martin was driving, which was a small mercy, but that meant she and JC had stopped to switch drivers, besides whatever else they'd done.

Well, they'd made their intentions pretty clear when they left the shop.

Because of where the dune buggy and Lynx's sedan were parked, Hannah couldn't pull into the lot. Instead, she halted in the travel lane. There wasn't so much traffic down 149 to make it a real problem. Since the obstruction was a police vehicle, there was no problem at all that *she* had to worry about.

Hannah and JC got out opposite sides of the van. She wore the serape over her shoulders by its concho clasps, though the afternoon was too hot for it.

JC cocked his flat-crowned hat precisely to shade his eyes. Compared to the local crowd around him, he looked like a broad-shouldered, slim-waisted video star. His jeans and silk shirt were an identical faded blue, separated by his dazzling silver belt.

"Deputy Martin," the Lynx snarled. "What was he doing in an official vehicle?"

"Running her through the paces, Marshal sir," JC said. "Checking her undercarriage for movement."

Ditsy shot an angry glance at me, but I just shrugged. JC was my brother, not my employee. There wasn't a thing in the world I could do about how he and the marshal got along.

"If you're not satisfied with my job performance, Lynx," Hannah Martin said, "then you'd better fire me. Otherwise—"

She shot an arm from beneath the serape and checked her watch.

"—I'll help you get the van back to the station, even though I'm not on duty for another half hour."

JC stretched ostentatiously. It made him look even taller and trimmer than he was in a normal stance. The Lynx, twice JC's age and forty pounds overweight, turned his head. He mumbled something.

"What?" said his deputy.

"Drive my car back to the station, Hannah," the old duelist repeated. He wouldn't meet her eyes. "I'll take the van. I want to try her myself."

He was walking toward the driver's side door before he finished speaking. Nobody got in his way.

The marshal gave the transmission a good test when he slammed the police van into gear. Hannah nodded to JC, no more, before she got into Feldshuh's personal sedan and whipped it in a tight turn to follow him.

JC smiled at the crowd. "Show's over, folks," he said brightly. He touched a belt concho, activating THE SQUARE DEAL's door. "Brian," he added, "I'll see you for dinner, then."

He tipped his hat toward Ditsy, then slipped into his car. Folks got out of the way as JC snaked THE SQUARE DEAL through the congested lot. The little car looked impossibly sleek against the dungarees and gingham of the local people.

Ditsy watched my brother go with an expression I

couldn't read. She turned to me and said, "Brian, do you want me to talk . . . ?" She nodded in Erculo's direction.

"No," I said. "I will."

Ditsy nodded and strode toward PRINCESS. I cleared my throat and said to my boss, waiting with a patience I didn't think I deserved, "Sir? I know I should work late tonight, but I have, ah, some business. I can come in early—"

Erculo gave me a broader smile than I had ever seen on his face. "Brian," he said, "I didn't expect you to be in today at all."

He touched the bandage on my right hand. "You shouldn't have been. Of course I don't expect you to work overtime tonight. There's nothing time-dependent left, not if Miss Wallace isn't concerned about her truck."

In relief, I let out the breath I'd been holding. That was true enough: nobody was going to be in a rush for repairs on the Spike-K vehicles—those few that could *be* repaired. And Big Ben's limousine was beyond salvage—not that he'd be needing a car any time soon, either.

"Besides," I said aloud, "you've got Joe and Mickey to help you."

Erculo snorted. The tow truck bumped around behind the shop with another shot-up four-by-four, this one so trashed that they'd had to dolly it in. It must have been one of those taken out by the police van's powerful missiles.

"Help?" Erculo repeated. "They'll do to finish the job they're doing, but . . ."

He looked back at me. "I thought repairing the marshal's van would take two days, Brian. It would have done, had you not come in today. No, you're welcome to your evening off."

Erculo's one eye slanted off toward town proper, though I

couldn't tell what he was really looking at. "Only, Brian . . . ,"
he said. "Be careful."

What did he know?

"I'm just . . . ," I said. Suddenly I felt angry. "I've just
got plans, Erculo. Look, I'm eighteen!"

He nodded, and smiled wanly, and lifted his cap to
knuckle his scalp. "Yes, Brian," he said. "And I have been
eighteen, which you think is old enough. I don't ask you to
be forty-seven. Only—be careful."

I thought for a moment that Erculo was going to say
more. Instead, he shrugged and said, "Come. We can finish
the inventory of this truck. I want to get in a parts order yet
today."

CHAPTER 15

"I'm going out," I said without looking over my shoulder at Mom and JC as I slung my grenade launcher. "I may be a while. Don't wait up."

Besides the clip in the weapon, I had only two reloads, so I stuck the fat cartridges in the front pockets of my shirt. I'd lost my bandolier the night before. Anyway, I didn't know how many grenades I'd shot off; maybe most of them. It had all happened in a blur with a few sharp images. . . .

Like Stannard Kames' frozen face.

"But you're not going tonight, are you, John?" Mom said. "Not tonight—you've been out every night since you came home."

"I reckon I'll stay here for a time, at least, Ma," JC said. I heard his chair scrape back from the kitchen table. "Might watch some television and relax."

"See you," I said as I pushed open the screen door.

"Don't do anything I wouldn't do, Brian, lad," my brother said with a chuckle like a cat's purr.

The night felt good. It was cool enough that I realized I should have taken a jacket, but I wasn't going back in to get one. The house was stifling when Mom and JC were together, and I don't just mean the temperature.

Ditsy and I hadn't set a time, so I figured to do like I always did—walk to the radio station when I was done with dinner. This night a car parked on Liberty Street started up and drove toward me before I was halfway to the center of town.

Normally I wouldn't have thought anything about that. Now wasn't normal. After the things that had been going on the past couple of days, I couldn't be sure there wasn't somebody laying for me to make a point or make a name.

Somebody's kin, maybe one of the Weatherspoon cousins from outside Welborn; or just a fellow who wanted to be known as the man who killed Deadeye Deal. There wasn't much skill in nailing a pedestrian without body armor from your car, but the survivor's the one who gets to tell the story.

I'd never had to think that way before, and I didn't half like to think that way now. I stepped well off the pavement, so at least I'd have the warning of the car's headlights slewing toward me—*if* he used forward-firing armament.

I wondered how it felt to be Lynx Feldshuh, with hundreds of kills over the years . . . or to be JC Deal.

The car pulled up alongside and started a tight turn that almost brought my grenade launcher to my shoulder before I realized the vehicle was PRINCESS. "Come on and get *in*, Brian!" Ditsy called. "Why are you jumping around like that?"

I stepped over the dune buggy's side rail and beneath the

horizontal hoop of its roll bar. PRINCESS could hold four people in a pinch, but the jump seats in back were over the rear axle and uncomfortable even on roads smoother than any near Mannheim.

"I didn't come to your house, because . . . ," Ditsy said. Her voice trailed off.

"I didn't expect you to," I answered.

Gear filled the back of the dune buggy, bungeed down to prevent it from coming adrift in hard riding. There was a suit of body armor to match Ditsy's own clamshell. It wasn't the one I'd worn the night before. I'd have been able to recognize that one from the scrapes I'd put in it skidding along over the ground.

"Put it on," Ditsy said as she brought PRINCESS up to the dune buggy's modest full speed as we headed back through town. "I brought you a case of forty-millimeter grenades—but if you want something else, other guns or more ammunition, we can stop at the store on the way and pick it up."

I started to say, *The hardware store's closed at this hour,* but I caught myself before I made that much more of a fool of myself. I forgot that this wasn't just Ditsy, this was "Miss Wallace"; to everything and everybody in Mannheim except me.

"No," I said. "I'll be fine. I'm better off with a weapon I know than trying to give myself on-the-job training when our lives depend on it."

I could've done without *that* thought, too. I'd been viewing this as a trip to Chalybeate Springs. How much more it could be hadn't been bothering me.

The ammunition was a mixed case of thirty rounds. Two of the three-round clips were flechette loads, which I'd never bothered with. It was just possible that we'd need the point-blank shotgun effect of the flechettes, but I wasn't likely to have one up the spout of my grenade launcher at the right instant.

The rest of the case was standard grenades: fifteen of them dual-purpose like the five I'd brought from home, and nine WP smoke. That meant Ditsy had noticed the way I'd used Willie Pete against the Spike-K personnel. I'd have figured her hands were too full with driving the truck to see anything else of what was happening.

Thirty-five rounds ought to be plenty. I wasn't likely to survive a firefight that burned up more ammo than that.

As well as the grenades and the body armor I struggled into while PRINCESS bounced over potholes, Ditsy was carrying a camera pack/ground station. "I thought," I said carefully so I wouldn't set off her temper, "we were going to look around Chalybeate Springs and come back."

"That's right," Ditsy replied. She drove expertly, straddling potholes wherever possible with short corrections on the steering wheel. "We're going to look over the Davidson and Sheen operation and film it for evidence. The camera sends its signal to the up-link—"

She nodded toward the back, though I already knew how the gear was supposed to work.

"—and that bounces it from a satellite to the receiving antenna at the studio. There's a record even if something happens to us," she added calmly.

I shivered. I really should have brought a jacket.

The clamshell's fabric covering had bellows pockets. I slid two loaded clips into each side and added the loose rounds I'd taken from my shirt so that I could put the armor on.

Lights were on at the shop as we hummed past. Erculo would be at it most of the night, if I knew him, stripping damaged plating from the TV truck. Fitting new armor was a two-man job; that would wait for the morning, when I came to work.

If I was alive in the morning. I'd seen too many people die to be sure I would live. I'd killed too many people myself to be sure I *deserved* to live.

Three tractor-trailer rigs boomed past us, bound for Mannheim. Two were independents, the third a Black Ball Packet. They were keeping close convoy and breaking their trip overnight when a week ago they might have driven on. The massacre the night before was the only news in Mannheim now, but the truckers remembered that somebody'd knocked off two rigs in two nights hereabouts.

I remembered the sheaf of hard-copy on previous incidents Ditsy had assembled. If there were no hijackings for the next day or two, the truckers would loosen up security again. Then there'd be a few more attacks; and a few more after the next pause.

And then the gang, because it had to be a large gang, would move on to another part of the country, hundreds of miles away . . . and start over. Until they were stopped.

I checked the chamber of my grenade launcher, making sure it was loaded, for maybe the tenth time since I climbed into PRINCESS. Ditsy was right about bringing her camera. The pictures she hoped for would be enough to bring down an Enforcement Group from the International Brotherhood of Truckers, whether the state government could be convinced to move or not.

"We won't take the local road to Chalybeate Springs," Ditsy said as she drove. "We'll leave the Interstate short of that and go overland. They're bound to have surveillance gear on the direct route if they're as organized as they seem to be.''

I frowned. "It's twelve miles," I said.

Ditsy tapped a module on the dashboard. I recognized it as a data-link to the ring of Global Positioning Satellites. I should have guessed: Big Ben Wallace's daughter could afford any equipment she wanted.

"You'll guide us in with this," Ditsy said. "You know how to use one, don't you?"

I nodded, then realized that she couldn't see me while she attended to her driving. "Sure," I said as I switched on the lighted moving-map display.

I could use it thanks to Erculo, who'd showed me how the system worked on a fully-equipped recreational vehicle we got in for repairs six months before. The RV's problem was its transmission had gone out, not battle damage—though Terry and the Pirates had amused themselves sniping at the tourists until we arrived in the tow truck. Maybe JC was right in what he did, and what I'd helped him do, to those kids. . . .

"And don't worry about the terrain," Ditsy added. "PRINCESS can handle it."

"I wasn't worried about the terrain," I said truthfully.

Ditsy reached over and patted my hand without looking away from the road. "I'm glad you're here, Brian," she said.

I didn't answer, but I guess I was glad, too.

Five miles past the junction of State 149 and the Inter-state, Ditsy cut off the dune buggy's headlights and pulled light-amplifying goggles over her eyes. Then she cramped PRINCESS's steering wheel hard right and we bumped north into broken scrub and grassland.

There was a quarter moon, plenty of light for the goggles, but it was going to make the trip a lot rougher. You lose depth perception through light amplifiers, so it's next to impossible to dodge potholes.

Ditsy was good, though I suppose PRINCESS's light weight helped the ride somewhat. I'd tested a few four-by-fours offroad, in broad daylight. I'd sure bounced around a lot more than we were doing now—even though I wasn't pushing, since they were customer's vehicles.

"You're a good driver," I said aloud. I was starting to relax again. I kept one eye on the map display. Despite twists and turns about obstacles, Ditsy kept us within 10° of the compass vector to our destination.

Instead of answering, Ditsy said, "Brian, what are you going to do? With your life, I mean."

"I . . . ," I said. "I . . . figure I'll work for Erculo. Maybe I'll . . . I mean, I'm learning a lot. I might have a shop of my own some day."

"Last night," Ditsy said. "I saw . . . how you did. You're really good. Have you thought of going on the dueling circuits?"

Stannard Kames stared at me as the concussion hit him like a trip-hammer and piano-wire shrapnel lanced through his face.

"No!" I shouted. PRINCESS lurched as Ditsy's hands twitched on the steering wheel.

"I'm sorry," I mumbled. "I—look, I used to think I wanted to do that, if only I had a car. But I don't. Maybe it would have been different if it was just car to car, but now that I've seen . . . No, I don't want to shoot people for a living."

"Does your brother talk to you about dueling?" Ditsy asked with her eyes on her driving.

"We haven't talked a lot since he got back," I said carefully. "Not any about that, no."

"But he is a professional duelist?" Ditsy said. Then she added, "Hang on," in the same flat tone of voice.

She turned hard left to square PRINCESS with the side of a gully. We plunged down, then accelerated up the far side in a cloud of dust and dirt clods. I grabbed my grenade launcher with one hand and the roll bar with the other, wishing I'd thought to buckle myself in.

"JC *is* a professional duelist, isn't he?" Ditsy repeated.

I realized I was talking to K660's star reporter now. "We haven't talked about that either," I said. "But—JC has money; THE SQUARE DEAL herself must have cost a fortune. And . . ."

I took a deep breath. "Terry and the Pirates, Ditsy, they were nothing. But if they really *had* been something, if they'd been pros, even, I think we would have taken them. I know, JC comes on like everybody's dirt compared to him and that irks you 'cause you're not used to it. But he really *is* that good, and the way he handles THE SQUARE DEAL didn't come from a simulator."

"That was about what I thought too, Brian," Ditsy said without inflection. "How far are we from Chalybeate Springs?"

There was more of Chalybeate Springs to see now than there had been a year before when I went through with Erculo on the way to Welborn. There still wasn't a lot.

Ditsy had brought a pair of light-amplifying binoculars. I used them while she panned the back of the community half a mile distant with the telefocus lens of her minicam. The miniature up-link in the back eeped as it transmitted the establishing shot to the satellite relay.

Chalybeate Springs was built along the west side of a gravel road that had probably had a county number back before the Troubles. Now it was just the Welborn Road. A new modular warehouse stood at the north end of town. The pale yellow-green amplification field of the binoculars showed me no doors or windows in the back and side in our direction.

Four frame buildings which had been stores twenty years ago were occupied again, though they were no longer in commercial use. The back door of one was open. By focusing carefully and raising the level of light intensification, I could see vehicles garaged inside. At this distance, I couldn't make out more than bodywork and the circular mass of wheels.

Patterns of red warning lights winked from the new thousand-foot antenna tower erected beside the southernmost building. We'd used it to navigate the last several miles. I'd have assumed the antenna was the base unit for Davidson and Sheen's communication with their delivery vans, but from what JC said the day before, they also monitored CB transmissions from a wide area.

Brush grew up to the backs of all the older buildings and was reclaiming the ground bulldozed in the course of erecting the new warehouse. Unless there were intrusion alarms—which I doubted, given the number of wild cattle wandering across the landscape—we could just about drive up to the back doors.

Ditsy set the minicam on her lap and put PRINCESS in gear. The terrain was generally rolling, but because the soil was so loose, our occasional heavy rainfalls created washouts of varied depth and extent. The dune buggy's four independently sprung wheels pumped and lowered to their suspension stops as Ditsy drove down into a gully six feet deep and almost twice that in width.

Clumps of grass and a few small woody plants grew from the walls and floor of the gully, but for the most part it was clear and easy driving. "We'll take this as far as it covers our roll bar," Ditsy explained. "Then we'll walk."

"Yes*sir*," I said.

She glanced at me sharply. I kept looking straight ahead, letting her guess whether it was a smart remark or not.

Which it mostly was. Ditsy was in charge, I wouldn't argue that. But I was a human being, not a piece of furniture, and I didn't *work* for her. I'd come along as a friend, not as a peon.

The gully took us up within a hundred yards of the four older buildings. That was stretching it a little, but PRINCESS's hull was below normal ground level and a thicket of Osage orange blocked vision from the direction of the town.

Ditsy unbuckled her seat belt and started to get out.

"Turn us around, first," I said.

She looked at me for a moment, then dropped into her seat again. It took her nearly a minute of backing and filling to reverse PRINCESS for a quick getaway. Maybe we'd leave as quietly as we came; but if we didn't, we were going to be in one heck of a hurry.

Ditsy got out with her minicam. She wore a holstered pistol, but that was just part of her clothing. I'd never seen her fire it or any other weapon.

I carried my grenade launcher, but besides it I rummaged in the dune buggy's tool kit and took out a tire iron and the jack. The jack was a self-powered hydraulic model, light-weight and very pricey—about what I'd expected to find in Miss Wallace's vehicle.

Ditsy looked at me funny. "What're you doing with that?" she asked.

"I figure we might be able to spring a seam of the warehouse and peek inside," I explained. "It's worth a try."

We headed first for the open back door, though. Music and occasional shouts came from the southernmost building, where a party was going on. When we were halfway to our goal, keeping low and edging from one clump of brush to the next, the back door of that building banged open with a louder spill of noise from the interior.

Ditsy raised up, pointing her minicam over the tangle of multiflora roses that hid us. I hissed at her to *get down*. She ignored me. I lifted to eye level also, so that I'd be ready if I had to shoot fast.

I wasn't wearing light-amplifying goggles—even if I'd had a pair, I couldn't have afforded to lose depth perception and peripheral vision. All I could see was three burly men, laughing and apparently having a contest about who could urinate farthest. After a few minutes they went back inside.

Ditsy ducked down. "Look at *this*," she hissed as she backed the recording, then set it to play through the minicam's external editing window.

The magnified images were clear, even on the camera's small screen. I'd thought the men were wearing shirts. Instead, they were naked to the waist but so heavily tattooed that they appeared to be clothed. One was missing an ear; the nose of another was so flattened that it took me a moment to realize what the fungoid lump in the middle of his face really was.

The man on this end of the group wore a belt made from motorcycle primary chain, plated with one of the noble metals to wink in the moonlight. I remembered the face of the tailgunner from the hijacked rig, mutilated by a weapon just like that one.

"*Those* aren't business staff!" Ditsy said. "That's a bike gang!"

"Let's see what's in the garage," I said, resuming my crawl toward the building that held vehicles.

The last ten feet to the garage had been bush-hogged clear. I glanced from the nearest cover, mostly milkweed stalks, in the direction of the party. Somebody might come out at any moment, but there wasn't any advantage in waiting.

I tensed to run. Ditsy darted across the open space a step ahead of me.

The atmosphere of the building was musty but sharpened by ozone. Davidson and Sheen—whoever or whatever the entity behind that businesslike name really was—had knocked out all the interior walls. Motorcycles and a pair of box-bed six-wheeled trucks were parked on the sagging wooden floor, out of the weather—

And out of sight. The trucks were nondescript, the sort of vehicles to load with loot transferred from a hijacked semi. The bikes—and a pair of three-wheelers, one of them equipped with a pod of nineteen 50mm rockets above the rider on a pivot mounting—were gang vehicles beyond a shadow of a doubt.

Ditsy's minicam purred. "Move out of the doorway," she whispered. "I don't want to turn on a floodlight, but the enhancement system has to have *some* illumination to start out with."

I stepped against the back wall, where I was out of the way. "I recognize that trike," I whispered back. "It was in the gang chasing the rig we watched be hijacked. One just like it, anyway."

Ditsy pointed the minicam at a bike amateurishly painted with flames and the name HELLBURNER in florid letters. "This one was too," she said.

There was a napalm tank behind the rider's saddle, connected by a hose to a wide-mouthed nozzle on the left hand-grip. I couldn't believe anybody was willing to ride with fifty gallons of thickened gasoline, waiting for the spark of a bullet's impact to set it off.

An owl hooted from somewhere in the rafters above us. I jumped out of a year's growth before I realized what it was. I was starting to get nervous. "Let's go," I said.

"First the warehouse," Ditsy replied. "Since you thought of the tools."

Yes, I had. Like a darned fool, I'd made sure we were prepared to go on instead of running for home like I *knew* we ought to do.

"Right," I said. "I left them back in the brush."

In the time it took me to find the jack and tire iron among the milkweed stems, Ditsy had already picked a spot on the side of the warehouse to try. I guess she figured it was safer to stay between the new building and the nearest of the old ones than it would be to be in the clearing at the rear when the next group of bikers staggered out the back from their party.

The warehouse was a simple structure built on a concrete pad. Its frame was a web of high-density plastic, covered with corrugated sheets of the same material. The sheets overlapped and were welded together along the outer edge of each overlap.

It wasn't hard to find a broken spot in a weld. I thrust the tire iron into the gap and levered it up and down, opening a wider separation. The sheeting was flexible. It tried to spring back into place even though the weld was broken.

When I had an opening a foot long, I managed to wedge the sheets far enough apart to get the jack between them. The powerful hydraulic motor whined as it ripped the welds further apart in both directions. By the time the jack was fully extended, it had split the sheets from the bottom on the concrete pad to higher than my head.

Lights were on in the warehouse, but there was no sound except the hollowness of a large building echoing with the tiny movements of its own structure.

"There," I whispered to Ditsy, proud of my success. "Wave your camera through *that* hole and then let's get out of here."

"I'm going inside," she replied as she unlatched her body armor and dropped it on the ground. "I'll fit."

I looked between the gaping sheets. The framework formed a pattern of diamonds a foot wide on the short axis and half again as high the long way.

"So will you," Ditsy added as she crawled through the bottom diamond, twisting sideways and pushing the minicam ahead of her.

I watched her disappear. "This is *crazy*," I muttered, to myself because Ditsy was already gone. Then I took off my own clamshell and followed her. I dropped two clips of grenades down the front of my shirt, the only way I had to carry such bulky ammunition without proper pouches or a bandolier.

Just in case.

The warehouse was climate controlled, though the air inside held the odor of lubricant and various less-identifiable smells from the goods stored here. I found Ditsy down an aisle of crates, filming the lot numbers on boxes of munitions.

She nodded toward the long, narrow cases which each held the motors for six 2.75-inch rockets. The warheads were boxed separately. "Those are from the second hijacking, I'm sure of it," she said. "Both the lot numbers and the manifest numbers jibe."

I looked at the end of a case more carefully. "Better yet," I said, "this one's got a Spike-K brand on it. They buffed it down, but you can still see how the wood's discolored."

Ditsy recorded the brand from several angles, hoping to get one where the light was right to display the evidence on a recording. She walked toward a right-angle bend in the aisle.

"Ditsy," I said, "I really think—"

She turned the corner and froze. I shouldered my grenade launcher, then jumped past her to cover whatever it was that had given Ditsy such a start.

It wasn't a biker, as I'd been afraid. It was a car.

The car was smoke gray and maybe a little larger than THE SQUARE DEAL. Except for that, it was exactly like the vehicle my brother drove.

CHAPTER 16

I remembered Erculo's discussion with JC in our front yard: *"A Komet, is she not?" "Actually, she's a Kormoran. Smaller . . . but you've got to see them together before you can tell the difference."*

This car was a Tempest Motors Komet.

It was backed against the rear wall of the warehouse. An aisle led directly to the double front doors, but a fiberglass screen shielded the sedan from any outsider who happened to glance into the warehouse while the doors were open.

The car purred. I walked around to the front and looked through the windshield. A massive vertical flywheel spun where the back seat should have been, but there was a distinct difference between it and the installation I had seen before. This disk was much thicker than that of THE SQUARE DEAL, but it was much smaller in diameter—so that the car's weapon could run the full length of the vehicle. This was the sedan

173

which had been murdering truck drivers for the past eight years.

The hijack gang couldn't take a car like this in for repairs to a fully equipped shop without arousing suspicion, and I knew from THE SQUARE DEAL that properly maintaining a Tempest Motors product took more skill than you were likely to find in a jackleg who worked for outlaw bikers. The nose panel that should have concealed the gun muzzle was missing, giving me a good look at the weapon.

The hole was only about an inch in diameter, but the walls of the tube were several times as thick. They had to be, not for strength but to contain the circuits which formed the powerful magnetic pulse.

"It's a homopolar railgun," I said, I guess to Ditsy though I kept staring at the weapon. "It converts energy from the flywheel into a jolt of electricity through the magnetic coils around the barrel."

The hole in the muzzle looked small, but it would pass a long rod of depleted uranium—at astronomical velocities. "A three-pound slug of DU," I figured aloud. "Accelerated to maybe 15,000 feet per second, a couple times faster than the highest velocity you could get from chemical propellants."

It was a military weapon, not particularly useful for a normal duelist. A fifty-ton tank could mount a flywheel and powerplant heavy enough to allow multiple shots. A unit small enough to install in a sedan could power only two or perhaps three rounds at the outside. The only sort of person with a use for a weapon like that was a murderer who intended to ambush truckers and kill them with single shots.

"It must have cost a fortune to buy this out the back

door of a military development workshop,'' I said, shaking
my head.

''They've *got* a fortune, Brian,'' Ditsy replied. ''They've
sold the cargoes of hundreds of hijacked rigs.''

Her minicam whirred. The plastic walls of the warehouse wouldn't block the signal from her camera to the up-
link, the way metal sheeting would have done.

''And don't assume they had to bribe somebody to buy
a railgun,'' she added. ''Davidson and Sheen is a legitimate
business, a *big* legitimate business. They fooled my father. I
wouldn't be surprised to learn they'd fooled a development
lab too.''

I stared down at the railgun's muzzle and shivered, remembering the trucker I'd had to mop out of the cab of his
rig. The weapon would deliver only a couple shots at a time,
until its flywheel was spun up again overnight; but those shots
were absolutely devastating to whatever they hit.

''Let's get out of here,'' I said as I stood.

''Brian,'' said Ditsy as she stared, I thought through the
driver's side window. Her voice was a croak.

I stepped over to her. ''Ditsy?'' I said.

The minicam was pointed at the frame above the window. There, black against the smoke-gray so I hadn't seen it,
was the name: THE CROOKED DEAL.

I lowered my eyes. The sedan's skirts were scabbed with
patches. They'd been shot up good. JC had mentioned a time
he lost control of his car because the skirts had been shot into
a colander and wouldn't hold him onto the road in a tight
turn. Now I knew what car he'd been driving when it happened.

''Let's go,'' Ditsy said quietly.

I grabbed her arm. "No, Ditsy," I said. "Let me—let me warn him, first."

She glared up into my eyes. I thought she was going to slap my hand away. "He's a thief, Brian," she snapped. "He's a murderer!"

"He's my brother," I said. I let go of her arm. "We'll smash the operation, Ditsy. You will, and I'll help you. But give my brother a chance to get away."

Her eyes stared at me and into me. At last she looked down at the sedan instead. "You're wrong, Brian," she said. "You're wrong as you can be. But we'll just report the car as part of the operation."

Ditsy shook her head violently, as if to fling a thought aside. "The authorities can come to their own conclusions when they arrive," she added softly.

Ditsy's left thumb wiped dust from the words, THE CROOKED DEAL. The car's alarm went off in a high-pitched electronic wail.

We both ran.

We made it to the gap in the warehouse wall together. "G'wan," I said, turning to face up the aisle we'd come from.

"No, you—" Ditsy began.

"Get out!" I snarled. All I could think of was the trio of bikers we'd seen, holding Ditsy and . . . "*Go*, you little fool!"

She wriggled through the gap and started to put on her body armor. Because I'd left my clamshell on the ground, I got into the cleared area behind the buildings before Ditsy did. I crouched behind my grenade launcher, but there was no one to shoot. We could hear the gang members running out of the far building, but they didn't realize we'd entered from the rear.

"Here they are!" someone bellowed. A powerful light blazed down the alley between the warehouse and the frame building beside it. I spun.

Ditsy was between me and the light. She scrabbled for her pistol. "Get—" I screamed.

A burst of shots knocked her across my feet. I heard the triple *whack!* of submachine gun bullets against Ditsy's breastplate and the sickening grunt driven from her lungs with her breath.

I squeezed my trigger, aiming by instinct. The flash of my grenade momentarily illuminated the biker while its shrapnel smashed the light in the fore-end of his submachine gun. I must have hit him squarely on the belt buckle, because glittering links of motorcycle chain flew out like sparks.

A couple gang members pointed guns down the alley and blazed away, but they judged it too risky to stick their heads around the corner and aim. Bullets riddled the warehouse wall twenty feet away.

Ditsy was moaning. She'd managed to rise to all fours. I grabbed her wrist, lifted her into a fireman's carry, and fired another grenade down the alleyway.

I didn't expect to hit anybody; I was just trying to keep the bikers' heads down. Somebody, either bolder than the rest or a latecomer who hadn't seen his fellow blown in halves by my first round, leaped into the center of the alley with a shoulder-fired rocket launcher.

I'm sure it was a rocket launcher because when my grenade hit his pouch of reloads, they went off in six different directions. The blast was staggering, even to me a hundred feet away. I used its push to start me and Ditsy toward cover.

We reached the shelter of the brush. Bikers were shooting down the alleys between each pair of buildings, but there was no danger to us in that. I heard vehicles start up in the garage, though, and that *could* be serious.

None of the bikes were real off-road machines, but the gang members were bound to have run on the dirt simply because there was so little else to do while they were holed up in a ghost town like Chalybeate Springs. A fellow who didn't mind breaking his neck could make pretty fair time cross-country on a motorcycle. I figured most outlaw bikers fell into the suicidal category.

Ditsy'd gotten her breath back enough to run instead of needing to be dragged. It was a good thing she'd stopped for her body armor.

It was a good thing I hadn't, since I'd have been hopelessly tangled in the clamshell when the submachine gunner started to shoot bits and pieces off me and Ditsy both.

She was holding the minicam in an instinctive deathgrip. Until I noticed that, I'd figured we'd both jump into PRINCESS and drive until the bikers caught up with us . . . as they surely would, seeing as the dune buggy was geared to lug up grades rather than for high speed.

But Ditsy's unit wasn't just a camera, it was a satellite communications suite—so long as the up-link in PRINCESS survived. I let go of her arm. "Hide in the briars!" I shouted. "Call for help! I'll lead 'em away!"

Ditsy wheezed something I couldn't make out. I pretty well knew what the words must be, but they didn't matter. My sudden plan was the only way either of the pair of us were going to survive this night . . . and anyway, bullet-bruised and burdened by her armor, Ditsy couldn't keep up with me as I sprinted the rest of the way to the dune buggy.

This time *I* was calling the shots.

Literally.

CHAPTER 17

I ducked into the driver's seat of PRINCESS as a burst of machine-gun fire snapped brush and leaves where my shoulders had been an instant before. Somebody was using a thermal sight, or he'd gotten real lucky. The tracers were red-gold, a beautiful color under other circumstances.

I switched on the dune buggy's motor. Before I floored the accelerator, I pointed my grenade launcher up at a 45° angle in the direction of the buildings and *choonk*ed out the last round so that I could reload one-handed with a fresh clip. I needed all the help I could get.

After all the point I'd made to Ditsy about turning PRINCESS around for a quick getaway, the first thing I did was to cramp the wheel hard and gun the dune buggy up the side of the gully in a tight turn that swung the nose toward Chalybeate Springs again. There was a lot of wild shooting going on. Headlights glared through the open back door of the garage building.

I wasn't familiar with PRINCESS's layout, but I'd driven a lot of vehicles for Erculo and found the weapons releases. On the dune buggy, they were caged buttons at the ten-o'clock, two-o'clock positions on the steering wheel. I thumbed up the left-side cage as I hauled PRINCESS around.

The biker with the thermal sight opened up again. His bullets cracked across PRINCESS's windshield. The internally lighted outline of the garage building's door starred and wavered as my Spalltex deformed. I squeezed the rocket trigger. The weapon's backblast cut a swath through the sumacs behind me.

A 2.75-inch rocket isn't designed to thread needles, and I'd fired this one without taking time to use even the dune buggy's rudimentary targeting equipment. All I needed to do was focus the gang's attention on me, so that they ignored the possibility a second intruder was huddled in a tangle of wild roses.

On the other hand, a row of buildings is a big target at a hundred yards. PRINCESS's nose was high when I squeezed off, but not quite *too* high. The streak of white exhaust intersected the wall of the garage, three feet above the door. For all the rocket had only a ten-pound warhead, it blew the whole end off the frame building in a bright red flash.

I wrenched the steering wheel hard right, reversing lock, in an attempt to use the rocket exhaust to screen my turn. That was probably a bad idea, since the expanding plume of white smoke was all most of the gang members could see. They laced it blindly with gunfire.

Bullets cut sumac stalks, hit both left-side tires, and spanged on the dune buggy's frame. One round hit my armored seatback so hard that it threw me against the steering wheel. If I hadn't been far enough into the turn that the plating was between me and the shooter . . .

A mounted biker rippled a pod of rockets into the night. Two of the seven straddled me. A blast twenty feet behind lifted PRINCESS's back end; then a streak and a red flash ten feet ahead froze an image of flying brush on my retinas.

I was in free fall. I thought I was dead, hit by a third rocket I hadn't seen, until the dune buggy slammed down again. I'd driven over the edge of the gully. It was cover and safety, but I almost threw the chance away. PRINCESS's right wheels ran up the far wall and nearly flipped me before I recovered control.

Headlights would be suicide and I didn't have night goggles. If there'd been time, I'd have grabbed Ditsy's.

If there'd been time and I'd thought of it.

My eyes flooded with purple afterimages of the explosions that had battered them. The tracers and shellbursts didn't help. I kept driving into the side of the gully even when I slowed PRINCESS to the speed of a fast walk.

It didn't really matter. I couldn't expect to escape. I just needed to keep the gang occupied until Lynx or whoever arrived to save Ditsy.

The bikers had gotten organized. Motorcycle headlights wobbled overhead, their halogen beams cut into harsh patterns by intervening brush. Two of the bikes had already gotten well out ahead on my flanks while I crawled along the gully floor. Several other vehicles were quartering the area outward from the town, moving faster than I could safely.

Somebody raced up and down the Welborn Road, making screaming shifts every time he changed direction. They weren't taking any chances of me making a fast getaway on the gravel.

I'd hoped the rocket hitting the garage had destroyed a lot of the gang's equipment. No such luck.

The flanking motorcycles revved together. They must be in CB contact with one another. The bobbing headlights crossed as the bikes started a run toward the gully from opposite sides, a couple hundred yards ahead of me.

The gang members knew the terrain. Rather than riding parallel to the gully, they decided to search that probable hiding place while airborne. The motors roared, then whined as both bikes left the ground and came down on opposite sides of the ten-foot gap with snarls and huge plumes of dust.

They were too far ahead of me, or vice versa; but when they jumped the gully once, they turned for another pass closer to Chalybeate Springs—and to PRINCESS. The vehicles working out from the buildings were getting nearer also, though I couldn't tell for sure just *how* near with nothing but motor noise and the quiver of headlights overhead to judge by.

It was time to do something besides run.

I heard the bikes coming. They would cross within twenty feet of me. I manually locked PRINCESS's automatic transmission in compound low, then uncaged the right-hand trigger button. As the motorcycles revved for another jump, I floored my accelerator pedal and lifted the dune buggy's nose in a dirt-spraying wheelie. At the peak of the rise, I squeezed the rocket trigger.

The motorcycles flashed above the gully, their timing as sharp as the blades of a scissors closing. The roaring white track of my rocket tore through the sky between them. I don't think it missed either bike by more than a hand's breadth. They cut the exhaust plume in perfect order—

And crashed in wild endos as they came down on opposite sides. The rocket hadn't hit anything but empty air, but the blast of its passage was enough to make the riders twitch. In a maneuver as tricky as the one they were attempting, that was all she wrote.

One of the bikes was HELLBURNER. The shock of impact triggered the flamethrower into the ground. Blazing napalm sprayed in all directions, including up into the cartwheeling vehicle. The fifty-gallon tank ruptured in a mushroom of flame that hurled bits of motorcycle across the landscape.

I didn't see what the other bike was doing, though I was pretty sure it was nothing survivable. I used my wheel-spinning acceleration to half climb the right-hand gully wall, then turned hard left and reversed direction back toward Chalybeate Springs.

That was about the best thing I could have done, because the sight of PRINCESS, bow-on and accelerating, spooked the sidecar rig following me down the gully without lights. The gunner jerked his trigger. The muzzle blast of the 90mm recoilless rifle was louder than Gabriel's horn, and the yellow powder flash was so close that the dune buggy's paint blistered, but the shell missed by inches. It detonated on the gully wall.

I was as surprised as the bikers were. There was no question of me shooting back. I tried to dodge, but my left front wheel bounced over the sidehack. PRINCESS climbed car, recoilless rifle, and gunner as if I'd run her into an unexpected boulder.

I heard screaming as I tore up the gully. PRINCESS handled okay, so I hadn't dinged the wheel rim or lost any suspension components.

When I'd scraped around the second twist of the gully,

I slanted both front wheels onto the left-hand bank and gunned PRINCESS onto level ground again. I thought I'd fool the bikers by that quick maneuver, but one of them was a lot too fast. He slewed his vehicle a hundred yards to my left. As the headlight flared over me and I struggled to aim my grenade launcher across my body one-handed, the bike opened fire with twin machine guns.

The guns were harmonized to intersect at fifty yards, so the streams of golden tracers were diverging again when they sleeted across the dune buggy. The back tire thumped and sparks ricocheted from the rear frame.

I twitched off a wild shot. As I did so, a piece flew from twelve o'clock on the steering wheel with a violence that made my left hand sting and jerk downward. PRINCESS spun wildly and stalled. I'd thought she was going to flip, but her active suspension justified its enormous cost by keeping the rubber side down despite the driver's screw-up.

A trike racing toward me from the other side of the gully rippled off three rockets that missed because PRINCESS skidded out of the line of fire. I ignored the vehicle controls for a moment and shouldered my grenade launcher properly in a two-handed grip.

The bike slewed on-target again in a cloud of dust like the one drifting downwind from my own sudden three-sixty. My grenade burst on his front tire before his twin machine guns opened up again.

The shaped-charge warhead blew out both sidewall and rim, causing explosive decompression. The bike went over in a low-side crash, so my second grenade hit either the rider or the powerplant just in front of the rider's crotch. Either way, he stopped being a problem.

Instead of restarting PRINCESS, I scrabbled behind the

passenger seat for the box of grenades. A frame building was on fire, but it was the one on the south end where the party'd been. Something big drove through the remains of the garage wall the rocket had smashed: a ten-wheeler was bumping toward me.

The trike with the rocket pod halted at the edge of the gully between us. The rider fired. The blast lifted PRINCESS's bow and stripped the treads from both front tires. The shock flung me bruisingly back against my seat. My fingers closed on a clip of grenades.

The rocketeer corrected his aim and blew me a dozen feet in the air.

The rocket hit just beneath PRINCESS rather than squarely on, and the dune buggy's skid plate was the heaviest armor the little vehicle had. The blast lifted me in a bilious somersault.

The ten-wheeler lumbering from the garage mounted a revolver-breech 20mm cannon in the cab blister. The gun had a high cyclic rate, 1,200 rounds per minute or better. The gunner, shooting as he drove, walked his fire onto the trike in a long, continuous burst that heated the cannon barrel bright yellow and burned every trace of rifling out of the bore.

The trike disintegrated under the stream of 8-ounce shells. A rocket lifted in a wild corkscrew. More of them exploded in the pod, but their blast was almost lost among the glittering shellbursts.

I hit the ground feet-first and rolled at least a dozen times. I don't know whether or not I lost consciousness, but if I did, it can't have been longer than a second or two. I was still holding my grenade launcher and the fresh clip.

My body didn't hurt. I could barely feel anything. I

locked the clip of grenades home in my weapon and stood up. The sky was reeling, but I didn't fall down.

There were fires scattered over the plain. The biggest came from the burning building. A spark of light merged with the motorcycle patrolling the Welborn Road. The bike blew up with a bang delayed by a half second or more from the flash.

Somebody'd gotten home with a missile, and it sure wasn't me.

I saw the ten-wheeler coming, but my brain forgot to tell my body to move. The vehicle swerved at the last moment and skidded to a halt beside me, throwing forward a choking cloud of dust. The headlights switched off. The cannon barrel was a sullen red torch above the cab.

"Brian!" Ditsy called. Her voice squeaked against my battered eardrums. She jumped down from the vehicle. "Brian! Are you all right?"

She grabbed me around the shoulders and started to hustle me in the direction of the buildings. I moved with her as soon as she got me started. "Come on!" she said. "Get away from the truck in case Lynx mistakes which one *we* are."

I saw the police van now. Its lights were off, but the backblast of a laser-guided missile illuminated the plume of dust the big vehicle raised from the gravel road.

I didn't spot the target until the flash of the warhead lifted the remains of a motorcycle and rider, both of them blasted into a number of small pieces. The van's missiles and thermal sights were a lethal combination with the Lynx or his deputy using them.

"Come *on*, Brian!" Ditsy repeated. "Are you all right?"

I looked at her. Submachine-gun bullets had blown three

divots out of her breastplate. I realized how frightened she must be—

And when I realized *that*, a fresh wave of adrenaline washed through my muscles. It was like waking up with a shower after a brutally hot day.

"Yeah," I said. I lowered my arm from Ditsy's shoulders to her waist, gave her a squeeze she couldn't feel through her clamshell, and released her to grip my grenade launcher properly. "I'll be okay now."

I nodded in the direction of the most recent explosion.

"Was that—?" I started to ask. *The last of them,* I'd meant to say, but that was stupid. Ditsy didn't have any better notion than I did of what was going on.

The motor of a rocket fired from ambush snarled, *"No."*

A wire-guided missile sprang out of a tussock of high grass, close to the road but about two hundred yards from me and from its target—the police van. The flare pot on the missile's tail undulated up and down as the gunner tried to acquire it in his tracking head.

I shouldered my launcher and fired without wasting time on laser ranging. The police van's front turret gunner was equally fast. The rocketeer was just outside the flamethrower's range, but the turret's coaxial machine gun laced the tussock with angry tracers even as I *choonk*ed my grenade off in a high arc.

Neither of us hit the biker, but we didn't have to. Either the blast of my grenade at the base of the tussock or the machine gun's muzzle flashes quivering in the tracking scope made the gunner flinch. The missile, as obedient to bad guidance as it was to good, sizzled skyward at a 20° angle. It flew harmlessly above the police van.

I blipped my range-finder for a precise follow-up shot. I

needn't have bothered. The co-ax stopped spitting and the van's front turret arched a brilliant flame rod into the tussock.

Water in the stems of grass and brush flashed into steam, blowing the tussock in all directions. The motorcycle, its concealment stripped away, stood in the white heart of the flame. The biker threw himself clear and stumbled blindly toward the road. He was a living torch. I waited for the van's gunner to put him out of his misery. The co-ax tracked the blazing man but didn't fire.

The motorcycle shrank as flames consumed its armor. The rider had placed his bike on its center stand for accuracy when he launched the missile. Both tires blew, spraying gobbets of burning rubber. The bike fell over. Small-arms ammunition in the saddlebags went off with a rattle and a series of multi-colored sparks glittering through the general inferno.

The biker continued to run. I fired. My grenade was a black spot against the flaming wrapper, then a white flash within it.

The biker fell backward on the gravel. His corpse still burned. The police van drove over the body.

CHAPTER 18

I waited with my grenade launcher pointed straight up—as non-threatening a posture as I could manage without tossing the weapon away. I wasn't ready to do that, even though all the recent dangers seemed to be dead or afire.

The van's fore turret traversed left and tracked us for a few seconds. The southernmost of the frame buildings was a hundred feet away, to our left front. It had burned to coals and charred posts, but the blazing buildings north of it threw a rich light over us.

The gunner recognized me—and more important, recognized Ditsy standing with her hand resting on my shoulder. The flamethrower's broad nozzle rotated 180° to point away.

I could see Hannah through the windshield, driving, which put the Lynx at the weapons console in back. The red-haired deputy wore her chicken vest of transparent Spalltex. For a change she'd donned an opaque stretch top beneath the armor instead of going for the bare-breasted look. The silver clasp of JC's serape winked from her throat in the dashboard lights.

Hannah slowed at the base of the radio tower, dark now that the warning lights had lost power. She turned deliberately so that the big vehicle completely blocked the road. I started to walk toward it. Ditsy came with me. I fumbled for her hand.

"I phoned the marshal through the station modem," Ditsy murmured. "He said he was on the way, and that he'd call in a posse from Welborn and Cross Creek."

She looked over her shoulder at the splotches of fire behind us, where the bikers had hunted me down the gully. HELLBURNER's pyre had expanded into a circle hundreds of yards across, but napalm still sputtered in the middle of it.

"I guess we don't need the posse," she said. She looked at me. "You didn't need Marshal Feldshuh, Brian."

"This isn't TV!" I said. I didn't mean to sound so angry. "I'm not some hero the bullets bounce off. *You* saved my life, Ditsy—when you came back with the truck. The Lynx saved both of us."

Flames had fully involved all four of the frame buildings. Ammunition cooked off at irregular intervals, spewing showers of sparks and an occasional glowing fireball.

A car came up the road from Mannheim, moving very fast.

Hannah stopped the police van. Its headlights bathed us for a moment before she switched them off, leaving the van a dark smear against the smoldering ruin of the nearest building.

The rear turret chuckled and clunked; the Lynx was reloading its empty chambers with fresh missiles. Both turrets swung to cover the oncoming vehicle.

"You kids keep outa the way!" rasped the marshal's voice from the loudspeaker mounted above the flamethrower. "Miz Wallace, I'm paid to keep your family safe. I'd appreciate you not making my job harder."

The oncoming vehicle slowed. The driver—he was only "the driver" for the moment—had seen the police van too late. He wanted to turn and run, but he knew you can't outrun a missile.

The chance of Lynx Feldshuh missing with a laser-guided missile was about the same as that of the corpse burning in the road getting up to have supper.

Hannah switched on the floodlight mounted above the rear turret. The tightly-focused beam lit up the newcomer 300 yards away. The vehicle was THE SQUARE DEAL, and the driver wore JC's flat-crowned, broad-brimmed hat.

Which is pretty much what I'd expected.

"Keep moving in, Deal," the marshal ordered through his loudspeaker. "And just in case you get a bright idea about what's possible, the whole missile rack's bore-sighted on you and we've got dual controls."

THE SQUARE DEAL eased closer demurely. I tried to jog toward the vehicles, but my body wasn't up to the increased strain. I was all right so long as I moved slowly. When I tried to increase the pace, I stumbled and fell. Ditsy clutched at my shoulders too late to help.

Twenty yards from the police van, JC turned in the road and stopped so that the vehicles were parallel, left side to left side. JC lifted his door and got out. He looked as calm as if he were standing in front of Wallace's Hardware, surveying the traffic on Liberty Street, instead of facing a flamethrower and a battery of missiles that could shatter even THE SQUARE DEAL's armor.

I got to my feet. Ditsy held me when I wanted to step forward again. I stayed where I was.

"Good evening, Marshal," JC called. His voice was clear and firm, loud enough to be heard over the continuing crackle of the flames. "We got a call at the house, from the TV station maybe, though I didn't catch the name."

He nodded toward Ditsy and me, as courtly as a duke. "Whoever it was said there was trouble up to Chalybeate Springs and Brian was in it. I hied myself here as quick as I could to help my little brother."

Hannah Martin had pulled the front seat's sighting hood down, now that the van was stopped. THE SQUARE DEAL's SLAP rounds might have penetrated the police vehicle's side plating, but the big machine gun couldn't possibly have killed both the Lynx and his deputy before one or the other of them fired an overwhelming volley of missiles.

It wasn't my doing. One of the gang members had phoned JC when the alarm went off. It was between my brother and the Lynx whether his lie about a call "from the TV station" would get him clear or not.

"You mean you came to pick up your other car, Deal," the Lynx replied. "THE CROOKED DEAL. I'd say it was too late for that. Matter of fact, it's too late for you."

I looked at Ditsy. I don't know what expression was on my face, but it backed her off like a slap.

"I *didn't* tell him about the car, Brian!" she cried. "I didn't! I just said the hijack gang was here at Chalybeate Springs and they were after us!"

The van's side door slid back firmly against its stops. Lynx Feldshuh stood in the opening, holding his big pistol in a two-handed grip. "I had the station engineer dump Miz Wallace's feed tonight to my console, Deal," he said. "On the way up here, I went over the whole thing. Plenty of evidence to hang you, even if we take time to hold a trial."

I stared at the grenade launcher in my hand. The police van's headlights flashed once. I looked up, startled. Hannah Martin's face was hidden by the sighting hood. She drew her left index finger across her throat in a warning made ghostly by the faint glow of the dashboard instruments.

"You're making a mistake, Marshal," JC said. I won't say he sounded worried, but there wasn't any energy in his denial. Those were just the words of somebody going through the motions.

"What's going to happen now, Deal," the Lynx said, "is I'm going to strip search you and put you in full restraints. Then we're going to take you back to town till Mr. Wallace recovers enough to decide what to do next. And if—"

The marshal's voice had lilted like a cat playing with its prey. Now it grew harsh again.

"—you think you might try something when I'm close enough to grab—don't. Deputy Martin can put a burst from the co-ax through your forehead before you can blink."

"Why, Hannah," JC said with a chuckle as cruel as a crow cawing while it probes for a dead calf's liver. He swept off his hat and bowed toward the cab of the police van. "You wouldn't do that and spoil my pretty face, would you?"

"Take your chances on the trial, JC," the red-haired deputy said through the loudspeaker. Amplification flattened her voice, but there couldn't have been much emotion in it to begin with. "You've got *some* chance there, at least."

"No, Marshal!" Ditsy cried. She darted forward. "Let him go for now."

193

"Ditsy!" I called, but I didn't know what to say next.

"I made a promise!" she said. She was halfway between me and the police van. I didn't know what to do or even what I wanted to happen. "In an hour, you can put out an alarm, but—"

"Miz Wallace—" the Lynx said. His pistol didn't twitch, nor did he turn his head, but his eyes flicked toward his employer's daughter.

That was all JC needed. He touched his index finger to the center of one of his belt conchos.

Hannah Martin's serape exploded. The bright pink flash blew the sighting hood away from her face in a millisecond before the face too vanished. The serape was woven from Fibrex, mixed with normal polyester yarns and dyed all the colors of the rainbow. The initiator must have been in the silver clasp.

JC didn't leave much to chance. He must have been planning for this possibility since the moment he arrived in Mannheim.

CHAPTER 19

The explosion was dull and echoing. It sounded like a firecracker going off in a garbage can, though hugely louder. The police van's plating withstood the blast, but everything within the armored box was pulverized and heated to several thousand degrees.

The shock wave staggered me and even my brother, though he knew what was coming. Ditsy fell backward. Marshal Feldshuh flew from where he stood in the side door like the cork popping out of a champagne bottle.

The pulse stripped off all the Lynx's clothing except for his body armor. Even the old duelist's boots and the shirt he wore under his securely-latched clamshell were gone.

As I rocked from the initial blast, air rushed back into the void and the van's interior gouted flames. Everything potentially flammable—fabrics, plastics, light metals, and the deputy marshal's pulverized flesh—burst into flame when oxygen reached it.

A bubble of fire puffed from the side door. Lesser plumes streamed through every other crack in the passenger compartment: ventilators, the co-ax port, and window frames strained by the Fibrex explosion.

The Lynx skidded face-first along the ground to where my brother stood twenty yards from the van. He was probably dead when he hit. JC slipped a flat, short-barreled automatic from the crown of his hat and made sure by shooting the marshal twice in the back of the neck.

Simultaneously with the second flat *crack* of the pistol, the van's napalm tank ruptured. The flamethrower's fuel and reloads for the missile launcher were contained in the rear third of the vehicle, separately armored to protect the crew from secondary explosions.

It was too late for the crew, so it didn't matter that the firewall failed in the opposite direction—admitting tendrils from the inferno within the passenger compartment to lick the napalm container.

Metal-enriched fuel involved the several missiles remaining within the armored box. Though the rear plating flew off as a gigantic blow-out vent, the blast kicked the tons of van several feet in my direction. Napalm sprayed in a fan a hundred yards from the vehicle. It clung to the grass and scrub, burning a brilliant red in which magnesium sparkled like meteorites flashing.

The triple explosions butted JC backward but didn't knock him off his feet. The gun that had finished Marshal Feldshuh swung—

Toward me, then—

Out to the side.

I was eighty yards from JC. That was too far for even my brother to be sure of an instant kill with a pocket pistol.

He knew it would have to be instantaneous, because I'd moved as quickly he did. The three dots of my sights glowed against JC's broad chest. He'd seen how good I was with my grenade launcher. At this range, I could just about kill him blindfolded. . . .

"Now lad, we've got a problem to solve here," my brother said, smiling across the grass toward me.

"*You've* got a problem, JC," I said. "I wanted you to get clear. But—not after what you did to h-h-Hannah."

"Lad—"

"Throw the *gun* down, JC," I said. "Throw it down now!"

"That's our problem, boy," JC said, as pleasant as if he was asking about the weather. "Look where I'm point—*don't* move, girl, or you'll lose a kneecap!"

My eyes flicked sideways. The explosions had thrown Ditsy down. She'd started to rise from her sprawl—turning JC's purr into the lash of a bullwhip.

"Don't move, Ditsy," I called. She was only twenty yards from the pistol's muzzle. I didn't doubt that my brother could put a bullet through her kneecap—or the bridge of her nose.

And I had no doubt at all that JC would do just as he threatened. When I looked at my brother, I saw Hannah Martin's startled, staring eyes lighted by a pink flash.

"As I pointed out, *boy* . . . ," JC said. "We have a problem."

"I'm not your boy, JC," I said. "I'm not anybody's boy."

He laughed.

The breeze lifted sparks in a rolling shower from the four frame buildings. Something touched the back of my neck and jabbed me, something hot or sharp.

I ignored it. I knew what I was going to do, now.

"Get into your car, JC," I said. "Drive away from here. But I'm telling you—when you brought Ditsy into it, you made it personal. D'ye understand?"

JC laughed again, a burst of sound as short and cruel as the shot that killed Tink Weatherspoon. "I guess I'll be able to sleep anyhow, boy," he said.

He backed slowly toward THE SQUARE DEAL, then paused beneath the open gull-wing door. We both knew there would be a moment as the door closed that Ditsy was safe but a well-aimed grenade could still find the opening. I deliberately pointed my grenade launcher up in the air.

JC threw himself into the driver's seat. THE SQUARE DEAL was rolling forward even before his door thumped closed. The smooth nose slid across me. The axial gunport was open.

I thought JC might fire, but that didn't happen. Maybe he was worried about ammo—15.5mm cartridges were special-order items in most hardware stores. Maybe he was afraid of what my grenades might do before he could let my life out through the neat holes his SLAP rounds would drill in my body. . . .

And maybe he didn't shoot because I was his brother. That's possible, but I figure it comes a bad third.

THE SQUARE DEAL pulled around the police van and accelerated north without headlights. JC must be using light-amplifying goggles. The dust of the car's passage rolled in twin vortices across the flames from the fan of napalm.

I was shaking. I knew what I was going to do, but it would be a moment before I was able to do it.

Ditsy ran to me. "It's over, Brian!" she said as she threw her arms around me. "The posses Marshal Feldshuh called from Welborn and Cross Creek, they'll t-take care of things. It's over!"

I hugged her rigid armor against me for a moment, then released her. "It's not over," I said. "But it's going to be."

I started walking toward the warehouse. Its fireproof roof and sheathing hadn't been damaged by the nearby conflagration.

"It's going to be over," I said. "Because I'm going to finish it."

CHAPTER 20

There wasn't any point in trying to get into the warehouse through the gap I'd forced in the siding. The opening was still there, but the frame building ablaze beside it was better protection than a minefield.

Besides, the front doors would have to be open for what I planned to do. I jogged up the road, past the fronts of the burning buildings. I had to thread my way past puddles of napalm, but the worst problem was the main fire. Heat pushed me to the far edge of the gravel. I didn't want to leave the road. Tussocks of grass smoldered internally, ready to cook my foot in an instant if my boot broke through the deceptively black crust.

Ditsy caught up when I was halfway to my goal. She was in better shape physically than I was, but she'd had JC's pistol pointed down the line of her eye. I don't think it sank in how close she was to death until THE SQUARE DEAL's door slammed and freed her from the threat. When she *did* have time to think about it, well, it slowed her down a mite.

"What are you doing, Brian?" she demanded.

I didn't answer. My mind was lost in the crackle of the flames, trying to make sense out of the noise. Sometimes I thought I heard voices, Jack Terry or Hannah or the biker who'd crashed HELLBURNER into his own inferno.

"Brian!"

The old Ditsy was back, bringing with her enough of the old Brian Deal to draw a response. "I'm all right, Ditsy," I said. "You wanted me here and I came. Now—look, just leave me be to take care of it."

The fireproof bulk of the warehouse shielded me from the heat that radiated from the burning buildings. It was like a bath in cold water. My head suddenly throbbed, and the breath of cool air I drew in seemed to displace boiling lava.

"But—"

I'd feared the doors would be sealed with a combination lock or even a thumb-print unit. There was nothing of the sort, just a control box with a rocker switch, connected to the drive motor by a conduit that ran up the exterior of the building. The only concession to security was a cage that could be padlocked over the switch. It wasn't closed, and a heavy screwdriver could have wrenched it away anyhow.

Davidson and Sheen weren't worried about *other* robbers; and since they moved their base every six months or so, there was no point in making a large investment in the plant. My brother was as ruthlessly efficient in his business decisions as he was when he went out to kill the people who might get in his way. Of course, that was part of his business too. . . .

I thumbed the switch. The motor whined to take up tension in the drive chain; then the doors clanked loudly and slid apart.

"Bri—"

"Ditsy," I said. I didn't know I was shouting until my voice echoed back from the hollow warehouse. "You started this, but now it's mine. Butt out!"

The floor of the warehouse was concrete, unpolished and scarred by the trowels which had leveled the surface in broad passes. It was good footing, even for somebody like me who knew he couldn't trust either his balance or his judgment.

I jogged down the central aisle. The screen that concealed THE CROOKED DEAL from the doorway was painted to look like a row of packing cases. I slid it out of the way.

The car's alarm system had shut off automatically after ten minutes. The muzzle of the big railgun pointed at my belly.

JC used the remote controls in his concho belt to open his car doors, but Tempest Motors provided manual latches. They were concealed by panels beneath the lower moldings. I knew where they were from working on THE SQUARE DEAL at the shop two days before, and I knew THE SQUARE DEAL's coded unlocking sequence also: 3-1-2, 2-3-1.

The code was the same for this smoke-gray Komet. That didn't surprise me. Otherwise, JC would have needed separate remote controls for his vehicles. The door of THE CROOKED DEAL lifted like the wing of a great bat, and I got in.

Even with the motor switched off, the sedan felt alive. The flywheel was balanced as perfectly as humans could create, but its motion still imparted a subliminal quiver to the car.

I turned on the power, then lowered the door to seal me into the vehicle. Instead of individual gauges, a video terminal angled toward the driver from the right of the steering wheel just like the dash of THE SQUARE DEAL. The initial setting of this multi-function display indicated battery charge was 100%, the flywheel spun at 100% of its optimum rate, and the built-in test program indicated wear of less than 7% on all moving parts including the tires.

There was a rotary switch on the side of the video terminal. I clicked it to the first detent. The display changed to a schematic of the car. The same wear data was noted by a sidebar and arrows to the affected parts, but there was a separate box—now empty—with the caption *Battle Damage*.

I rolled the switch again. I thought it would return to the initial display. Instead, the video screen gave me a crisp window from a camera speeding down a gravel road bordered by rolling scrubland.

For a moment, I couldn't imagine what I was seeing. Then I realized that this was a light-enhanced image transmitted from THE SQUARE DEAL. I was watching JC's getaway through pictures sent remote from a camera mounted on the hood above the muzzle of the 15.5mm machine gun.

I took a deep breath. The car was ready to go. All it needed was for me to find the courage to put it into gear.

I set my grenade launcher on the passenger seat across the central console that shrouded the railgun's barrel, turned on the headlights, and slipped the selector into *Drive*. Taut, perfectly balanced, and throbbing with enough power to open truck plating like a can of sardines, THE CROOKED DEAL obeyed my directions.

Ditsy stood beside the warehouse doorway, watching me without speaking. Her face was pale in the pure white glare of my headlights.

Then I was past and alone except for the thrum of gravel beneath my tires. The road stretched forward like an enlargement of the image on my video display.

CHAPTER 21

I wasn't pushing hard. I didn't know the machine yet, and I had no desire to catch my brother before he met the posse anyway.

The most important thing about the Komet's handling was that it did exactly what I told it to do through the controls. Steering was as precise as a razor cutting meat, and only the anti-locking circuitry kept me from spinning out the first time I tapped the brakes going into a curve and misjudged the available braking power.

Armor, flywheel, and the railgun itself made THE CROOKED DEAL extremely heavy for its size and slowed its acceleration. Even so, the sedan came quickly and smoothly up to as much speed as I felt comfortable with on this gravel.

The remote image of my video display changed abruptly. The road dipped and swept upward again at frequent intervals. As THE SQUARE DEAL crested a gentle rise, the farthest horizon brightened. A van and a pickup lifted over the distant hill, side by side.

The Welborn-Cross Creek posse had arrived. The headlights of following vehicles silhouetted the leaders.

I drove with one eye on the road and the other on the remote display. JC can't have known the marshal had called in help, though I don't guess it was too big a surprise.

I kept waiting for the image to do a quick one-eighty that would put my brother back heading south as fast as he'd driven away. Instead, the video from THE SQUARE DEAL eased down into a swale and up the slight rising curve. Light haloed the next crest, gleaming through the interstices of grass and sumac stems.

The windshields of the posse's leading vehicles humped faintly above the hilltop. The van's headlights appeared a half second before those of the pickup to its left. The view in my video display shifted minusculy to the right, then blurred with smoke and vibration as THE SQUARE DEAL's machine gun fired a two-second burst.

The posse had put its heaviest vehicles in the lead. That didn't help. The impact of twenty-odd high-velocity penetrators, concentrated in an area no bigger than a man's hand, was more than any windshield could withstand. The van swerved to the left as projectiles and spiky fragments of Spalltex armor pulped the driver's chest despite any body armor he was wearing.

The van flipped. A following vehicle smashed into it with a flash that warned of fire.

The pickup beside the van in the front row mounted a 106mm recoilless rifle on its cab. Instead of an optical or electronic rangefinder, the heavy recoilless used a coaxial machine gun for aiming. The gunner laced the night with a thread of golden tracers, reaching for THE SQUARE DEAL. When the machine gun bullets ricocheted from the armor of his dim, white target, he fired his main gun.

JC was already slewing THE SQUARE DEAL to bear on the pickup. I saw the image of the recoilless rifle's backblast flare through the haze and vibration of the 15.5mm machine gun.

The pickup spun out when its driver jerked the steering wheel as he died. The recoilless rifle jolted THE SQUARE DEAL with a direct hit. Saturated red light flooded my video display.

At first I thought the quickly shifting images following the flash meant that THE SQUARE DEAL had been blasted out of control. A moment later I saw that JC had merely turned. He was headed back southward through the settling dust of his previous progress.

He'd won the skirmish and stopped the pursuit in its tracks, but the brief fight had cost a third of JC's meager ammunition supply. There were half a dozen vehicles in the posse besides the pair he had destroyed. THE SQUARE DEAL couldn't slug its way through such a mob and it couldn't run cross-country. That left JC no option but to head south and hope to reach the Interstate.

JC had been lucky. A sedan, even one with armor as thick as that of THE SQUARE DEAL, couldn't shrug off the shell of a one-oh-six. The gunner had loaded with a squash-head projectile, designed to spread over the surface it hit before exploding. The pressure pulse, amplified by reflection within the armor, would spall jagged chunks off the inside of the plate.

But the shell had struck THE SQUARE DEAL's smoothly-sloping hood at a very flat angle of incidence. The explosive charge ricocheted before the base fuze detonated it in a huge, harmless flash above the sedan.

Both JC and I had been lucky to survive some of the things that had happened this night. I wondered whose luck was going to hold.

THE CROOKED DEAL was rock solid, a pleasure to drive even on as bad a road as this one. My brain concentrated on the rhythms of broad, sweeping curves and of hills and swales as gentle. It kept me from thinking about what would come next—

Until it came, with a sharp rush that dissolved my fatigue in fresh adrenaline.

JC was running without headlights, but I saw the glow of *my* lights coming from a distant rise on the remote display. An instant later, a buzzer sounded from my dashboard. White letters on the display overprinted the image of my headlights with LASER! LASER!, warning me that sensors in the skin of THE CROOKED DEAL were being painted by JC's range-finder.

Before I could react, the warning cut off and my headlights dipped out of the sight of my brother's car. I sped downslope, bumped across a rocky bottom swept clean by freshets when it rained, and started up the next hill.

I knew what was coming next. I'd seen it happen to the posse.

My headlights swept a broad patch of grass and chicory at the roadside. The flowers were a rich blue blur as I accelerated, fighting the desire to brake to a screeching halt while I was still beneath the brow of the hill. The video monitor brightened, then flashed LASER! while the buzzer sounded and I ducked across the console.

JC knew who was driving the car coming toward him. I thought he might give me a warning, a single round or two that he knew would only craze the thick windshield of THE CROOKED DEAL.

Instead, he put his 15.5mm gun on high rate. He'd reloaded with depleted-uranium ammo. The gentle slope gave JC three seconds as the cars closed. The stabilized laser sight and the low-dispersion mounting punched sixty or more DU rods into the same tiny point—right in front of where my nose should have been.

The windshield of THE CROOKED DEAL blew inward, showering me with stinging bits of Spalltex. The SLAP rounds hit the transparent armor with a sound sharper than a burst of submachine-gun fire. The penetrators glowed from friction heating as they tumbled across the interior of the car to bury themselves in the headliner. A few of them hit the flywheel and ricocheted wildly, spitting red sparks.

I threw THE CROOKED DEAL into a spin by hauling the steering wheel hard right without rising to look over the dashboard.

If things went wrong, I was going to collide with JC's car at a combined velocity that would total even a pair of Tempest Motors sedans. I had to take the chance: this was the only scenario that would convince my brother that he'd killed me. I figured JC was a good enough driver to dodge a spinning obstacle. He'd had a right plenty of experience, or I missed my bet.

THE CROOKED DEAL swapped ends at least three times. I could tell when we were pointed north by the blast of air punching through the fist-sized hole in the windshield.

Light flooded my windows—not JC's headlights but my own, reflecting from THE SQUARE DEAL's white side as it roared past the nose of my smoke-gray sedan at a distance of inches or less—

But past.

Only then did I sit up straight in the seat and brake hard. THE CROOKED DEAL ran off into the chicory before I got her under control and pointed southward. I lost some paint and dinged the left quarter panel, but there weren't any ditches or boulders that might have disabled the car.

I accelerated again, uncaging the spoke-mounted weapon switch with my left thumb. The trigger ring within the steering wheel glowed green. Wind buffeted, but the hole the fifteen-point-five chopped was a clear window in the middle of a frame of pressure-distorted Spalltex.

My right hand reached up to the headliner and swung the targeting lens over my right eye. I centered it on the white glow of THE SQUARE DEAL and clicked on the stabilized laser. I had a perfect, zero-deflection shot at the back of my brother's car—and he knew it, because his sensors warned him of the targeting laser just as mine had done.

If JC had been on a hard-surfaced road, he might have spun to engage me. He knew he couldn't do that on gravel where he couldn't suck a vacuum into his skirts. If I fired my axial railgun, the only question was whether the depleted uranium slug would splash directly through his body as similar rounds had done with so many truckers, or whether his flywheel would shatter at the impact and ream out the sedan's interior with a sleet of sharp-edged fragments. The flywheel acted as additional armor until its massive integrity was breached; then it became a bomb.

I don't know if I would have fired. I don't think my brother knew either . . . but he knew that he didn't dare take the chance. He stood on THE SQUARE DEAL's brakes.

The white car rotated more than 120° counterclockwise, spewing up a wall of dust as the tires skidded broadside across the gravel. My thumb closed over the trigger button. I thought he was trying a bootlegger turn without the skirt's vacuum to aid him.

The pearl-white sedan came to a halt with its nose and machine gun aimed off into the prairie. The driver's-side door rose. JC got out, moving with casual smoothness in the glare of my headlights.

I tapped my brakes, slowing cautiously with the railgun's bore centered on JC's belt buckle. I stopped thirty yards short of THE SQUARE DEAL's front bumper. My brother took off his hat, ostentatiously removed the pistol from its concealment in the crown, and tossed the weapon into the scrub.

"All right, Brian," JC called. His voice was muffled by the armor surrounding me. "Very slick—I'm proud to be your brother. But what do we do now, lad?"

I opened my door, waited a moment, and then got out with my grenade launcher pointed at JC. There was only one round left in the clip, but he didn't know that. One round was plenty for what I had to do—

If I did it.

"Now we wait, JC," I said. My knees were shaking, but the launcher's three-dot sight lined up solidly across my brother's chest.

"You really out-thought me, Brian," JC said. He rubbed the knuckles of his right hand across his cheekbone. "Of course, if I'd known it was you, I'd never have shot. A brother wouldn't kill a brother, Brian."

He lowered his hand toward his belt. "Don't *try* me, JC!" I shouted.

He froze where he was. For all his seeming nonchalance, JC was as tense as I was.

"If we wait for those yokels from north of here to get

some courage back, lad,'' he said, ''then they'll come down and hang me. That'd be murder, Brian. You wouldn't murder your brother.''

''There'll be a trial, JC,'' I said. Something was wrong, but I couldn't tell what. I heard a quaver of uncertainty in my voice. ''That's more than your girlfriend got, Hannah Martin. Or any of the truckers you killed.''

Headlights gleamed on the road from Chalybeate Springs. I heard the rumbling motor of a heavy truck. I didn't care who came to take this responsibility from me, only that someone had to come soon.

JC heard the sound also. ''Brian, think what Ma would say if you—'' he began.

I knew what was wrong: THE SQUARE DEAL was moving. Though the sedan appeared to be shut down, the flywheel fed power through a creeper gear. The vehicle was crawling around in a continuation of the turn that would bring the nose—and the machine gun—to bear on me. It was one more of the automated features that made THE SQUARE DEAL so lethally special.

Without consciously thinking about it, I shifted my point of aim. JC saw the motion and threw himself down.

I fired, a perfect shot. My grenade ticked the doorjamb and burst inside the sedan, riddling the controls with fragments.

I don't know whether it was a short circuit caused by the grenade or JC himself, stabbing at a silver concho, that triggered THE SQUARE DEAL's machine gun. My brother was in the air, rolling to get clear of what he thought was a grenade aimed at him. He was almost touching the muzzle of his gun when it fired.

I remembered that as JC killed Tink Weatherspoon, he'd

chuckled that SLAP rounds would do in a pinch for anti-personnel use. These did. The long burst cut my brother's slim, handsome body almost in half.

The truck from Chalybeate Springs pulled up behind THE SQUARE DEAL. It was the hijack vehicle Ditsy had driven from the burning garage while I fought the bikers. I wondered if she'd reloaded the blister cannon before she followed me.

Ditsy leaned from the side window. "Are you all right, Brian?" she called.

THE SQUARE DEAL's upholstery began to burn. I could probably smother the flames if I tried.

I didn't move. Fire was the best thing for the car that had brought the monster my brother had become back to Mannheim.

"I'm fine," I said.

I flung my grenade launcher into the darkness. "I'm fine!"

THE BEST IN
SCIENCE FICTION